A NIGHT TO DIE FOR

A NIGHT TO DIE FOR

WITHDRAWN

LISA SCHROEDER

Underlined

Text copyright © 2022 by Lisa Schroeder
Title page illustration copyright © Rumdecor/stockmamba.com
Cover photo © 2022 by Juan Moyano/Stocksy

All rights reserved. Published in the United States by Underlined, an imprint of Random House Children's Books, a division of Penguin Random House LLC, New York.

Underlined is a registered trademark and the colophon is a trademark of Penguin Random House LLC.

GetUnderlined.com

Educators and librarians, for a variety of teaching tools, visit us at RHTeachersLibrarians.com

Library of Congress Cataloging-in-Publication Data is available upon request.
ISBN 978-0-593-48153-0 (pbk.) — ISBN 978-0-593-48154-7 (ebook)

The text of this book is set in 11.25-point Adobe Caslon Pro.
Interior design by Andrea Lau

Printed in the United States of America
10 9 8 7 6 5 4 3 2 1
First Edition

Kelly Hager—
I appreciate your unwavering support so much.
This murder is for you!

A NIGHT TO DIE FOR

Hey, Josh,

Excuse my scribbles. Prom awaits, as you know, and I need to get ready, but I can't stop thinking about discovering you around the corner last night. I know you heard things and you're probably thinking I've lost my mind.

But I promise, I'm fine. Pissed at you for listening in on my phone conversation? Absolutely. However, I know we do stupid things in the name of love, so I forgive you. This time.

I'm sure my attitude lately has you worried. But please, try to understand what your diagnosis, and everything that came with it, did to me. It tore me apart. It broke me. I tried to stay strong. But you're my little brother, and when I saw up close how fragile life is, it messed with me. Yes, you're better now and it probably doesn't make any sense that I can't just go back to "normal."

The thing is, maybe "normal" is a big, fat lie. Or maybe it doesn't apply to me.

I know I'm hard to love sometimes. And I'm sorry for that. But please believe me when I say: I'm fine. And when tonight is over and tomorrow comes, I'm going to be so much better than fine. You just have to trust me.

Can you do me a favor? Don't say anything

to anyone about what you heard last night. I will reveal all to you soon, I promise.

Our secret for now, okay? People wouldn't understand. I REALLY don't want to be "that girl."

> Love you to the moon and back,
> Mirabelle

Jason @jajumps23

Congrats to our prom king & queen, Mario and Mirabelle! @luigifanboy and @belleofwillow, hope to see you at my house later to celebrate. #royaltyinvite

---

Lucas @lucaspucas

Are you kidding me? @luigifanboy is prom king? I wish I'd been there to see that. Congrats, Mario!

Eva @evadeva

OMG, that was so funny. Did you see @luigifanboy's face when he realized his crown had worms in it? Someone better have video.

Donny @DonnyB43

You want video? I've got video! #funniestprankever

Elana @elanadex

How come @belleofwillow didn't have anything weird going on with her tiara? Is it because she's the one who did it? I wouldn't put it past her.

Mirabelle @belleofwillow

Hey @elanadex, Mario loves worms. Just ask him. And by the way, keep your mouth closed up tight if he tries to kiss you. Otherwise you'll get way more than you bargained for.

Elana @elanadex

@belleofwillow ???? Ew!

Mario @luigifanboy

Uh nope @belleofwillow I never said I love worms.
And that was a long time ago. Maybe I've changed.

Parker @parker_brands

What are you talking about @belleofwillow?
Something you need to tell me?

Mirabelle @belleofwillow

@parker_brands It was a long time ago. You and I
have bigger things to worry about. Trust me.

Parker @parker_brands

@belleofwillow Looks like the ride over to
@jajumps23's house is gonna be a fun one.
Can't wait to hear the story.

Mirabelle @belleofwillow

Remember friends, the truth will set you free.
Holding tight to that thought tonight.

Lucas: Dude. What is happening?

Mario: When the principal put the red velvet crown on my head, I felt things crawling in my hair. Unbelievable!

Lucas: Sorry man. But hey, the prince of intellect and the princess of imagination became prom king and queen.That's pretty lit.

Mario: I think she did it. Mirabelle. The worms, I mean. Smh our dance was awkward af. And then on top of that, she decides to bring up our stupid kiss from years ago on twitter? Shit.

Lucas: The video is going viral, man. You're gonna be famous.

Mario: I think I'm gonna be sick. I looked like such an idiot.

Lucas: You think she targeted you? How'd she know you'd be the one chosen king? Wouldn't she have wanted her prince of charm Parker to get it along with her?

Mario: No clue, but I wish he'd gotten it. It's not like I wanted it. Hey, gotta go. People are leaving for Jason's party now. Wish you were here, man.

Lucas: Hang in there. See you tomorrow? I want to hear about it.

Mario: Yeah. See ya.

MARIO

A car approaches. But not just any car. When he
spots me, standing next to my little Nissan pickup, he turns
on his flashing red and blue lights.

There isn't much traffic out here, especially late at night. No
houses nearby either. This section of Wessinger Road has just two
lanes and then grass with lots of tall fir trees farther back. The
ditch is a few feet deep, and that's where the girl's body lies, fully
clothed in a red dress and heels. My whole body is shaking. I take
a deep breath and roll my shoulders back, telling myself to relax.

The deputy gets out of the car and shines a light on me. "You
all right, son?"

I cross my arms in front of my stomach and hope I can keep
it together. "I was driving by and saw something in the ditch. I
couldn't tell what it was. I got out and shined the flashlight on
my phone down there. Just as I saw it was a girl, you pulled up."

The beam from his flashlight moves from me to her. "Oh, no."
He starts running down into the ditch. He yells up at me, "You
sure you didn't hit her? With your vehicle?"

"No. I mean, yeah. I'm sure! I didn't hit her, I swear," I call
back. "I just found her there."

He's down there for only a minute before he's radioing for help. "Dispatch, I've got a female juvenile and she's unconscious with no pulse. Send medical, code three and extra units. Location is Wessinger Road, just south of Hart Road. Her skin is tacky. I'm starting CPR."

I pace the side of the road. Back and forth. Back and forth. I keep wondering if there's something I should be doing, but he told me to stay put.

After a few minutes have passed, I yell out, "Is it working?"

He doesn't answer.

A minute later, I hear the sirens. A fire truck and an ambulance pull up, and a few seconds later, another deputy. I stand back and watch as everyone moves into action.

When the original deputy climbs back up the steep embankment a while later, he's breathing hard. "Dispatch, page out detectives," he says into his shoulder mic.

"Is she dead?" I ask. I read his name tag: Deputy Mitchell.

He wipes his brow as he replies. "Yes." He circles my truck, his flashlight zooming in on every little dent and scratch. The beam finds Elana, my prom date, curled up in the front seat. She doesn't even stir.

"Oh, god," I mutter. I hold my stomach tighter. I can't believe this is happening.

The other deputy goes to work taping off the scene with crime tape.

Deputy Mitchell pulls out a notebook. "Can I see some ID?"

I pull out my wallet and hand him my driver's license. After he writes my information down, he says, "Step over here with me, please. Away from your vehicle." I follow him over to his car. "Who's the girl in your truck?"

"My prom date. Elana Dexter. She's kind of, um, out of it, at the moment."

"Too much to drink?" he asks.

I don't want to tell him, but he'll check for sure no matter what I say.

"Yes."

"Just broke up a party not too far from here. You two go to a party tonight after prom?"

"Yes," I say. "How'd you know?"

"Neighbor called it in," he says. "Said it was getting noisy. So, what about you? Have you been drinking as well?"

"No."

"Can you tell me what happened tonight?"

"We left the party and Elana didn't want to go home right away. Didn't feel well, you know? So I drove around, she passed out, and then, like I said earlier, I saw something in the ditch, so I stopped."

"Looks like the deceased came from prom as well," he says. "Didn't find any ID on her. Any chance you might have been able to see her face well enough to identify her?"

"Yeah. She goes to my school. Her name's Mirabelle Starr."

I want to say, *She's the girl I stood beside onstage just a few hours ago when we were crowned king and queen.* I can't believe she's dead.

"You sure about that?"

"Positive."

"Did she have a date for the prom?"

"Yes. Parker Young is her boyfriend."

He finishes up his notes, then reaches around and opens the back door of his car. "Mario, I'd like to have you take a seat back here. I'm going to need to get a Breathalyzer test, and then a detective will want to talk to you."

"Okay."

After he gives me the Breathalyzer, which comes out clean, he tells me to hang tight. And so I do. I call my mom to tell her about finding Mirabelle and what's happened since and that I hope to be home soon. She's worried, of course, but there's nothing I can do. After we're done talking, I sit back and wait while watching the commotion outside. More cops arrive, including a state trooper, and the road is completely blocked off on both sides. At one point, I see Deputy Mitchell talking to Elana, who's finally woken up.

A while later, a different deputy pops his head in. "Just have a few more questions to ask you. He'll be over in a few."

"Do I get to go home soon?"

"Hopefully it won't be much longer."

One of the patrol cars pulls out and drives away.

"Where's he going?" I ask.

"To the victim's home," he says softly. He looks up at the sky, like he's trying to keep tears back. "Every year, parents worry about their kids on prom night. Hoping and praying they keep their wits about them. Hoping they don't do something crazy and end up in a ditch somewhere." He shakes his head and looks in the vicinity of Mirabelle. "What a tragedy."

PARKER

've never gone into Grandma and Grandpa's liquor cabinet. Never even thought about it. Until now, that is. I know it's not going to magically cure my broken heart, but I just don't know what else to do. If you're a musician and someone breaks up with you, I guess you grab your guitar and write a song. But what do normal people do? I don't have a clue, so it's tequila for me.

I'll try anything to stop the memories from coming fast and furious, like they are now.

It was our junior year and we both landed parts in the spring production of *The Lion, the Witch, and the Wardrobe.* Mirabelle was a fun, wacky girl who loved to make people laugh. Her exuberant personality slightly intimidated me at first. I consider myself outgoing, but not like her. Though, really, no one's like her. Anyway, she loved to joke around with her castmates, and eventually the joke was on me.

I played the part of Ginarrbrik, the White Witch's dwarf. During dress rehearsal, in the scene when the White Witch and the dwarf first meet Edmund, I was following the script by pulling a book out of my coat to look up the word *wardrobe.* Inside the book I discovered a picture cut out from an old *Playboy* magazine.

It took everything I had and then some to stay in character and not burst out laughing. Belle, a cute little thing, played the part of one of the beavers, so she was offstage at the time. Of course, I didn't know for sure that she'd done it, but I had a pretty good idea based on things I'd heard about her.

Later, when we were standing around waiting for rides, Mirabelle came over to me with a big grin on her face.

"Hi," she said.

"Hey." I pointed to a book in her hand. "What are you reading?"

I can't remember the title now, but she told me what it was and said it was an epic fantasy about a dragon hunter named Gretel.

"Oh," I said. "The poor dragons."

"Yes. The handsome king wants them gone."

"But the dragons were probably there first. Let me guess: Gretel and the king eventually fall in love."

"Yes," she said. "But not in my version. In my version, she kills the king, and the villagers appoint her queen, and she is able to learn dragonspeak and control them. The dragons live another day."

"What do you mean, your version?"

"I write fan fiction," she explained. "Online. You've read fan fiction, right?"

"No," I said. "Never have."

"Oh, well. Poor you, then."

I decided it was time to see if she'd come clean. "So that's what you do when you're not messing around with actors' props, huh?"

A smile crept across her face. And then she started laughing.

See, the thing is, when my girl Belle laughed, for that brief moment, it felt like being nuzzled by a litter of furry puppies. Like standing outside at midnight and witnessing a glorious meteor shower. Like eating a warm piece of homemade apple pie topped with caramel sauce and vanilla ice cream.

She reached out and squeezed my elbow. This was something she did a lot, I discovered. I don't know what it was about elbows that she liked, exactly, but that's usually what she reached for when she was talking to someone.

"You're not mad, are you?" she asked as my elbow rejoiced.

I wanted to say, *How could anyone be mad at someone who makes you feel like you're being nuzzled by a litter of puppies?* But I didn't. I just said, "No way. It *was* pretty funny. Where'd you get it, anyway?"

"My dad has a few," she told me. "He calls them 'collectors' items.' I call them disgusting sexist misogynistic rags."

"That are good for a laugh at a poor actor's expense?"

"Exactly," she said, her green eyes sparkling like whitecaps on the ocean.

From that moment on, Mirabelle Starr became the person I thought about before I went to sleep at night, when I woke up in the morning, and during the hundreds of minutes in between. Until I met her, I did my best to live in imaginary worlds. Through movies. Through art. Through books. Through plays. What I love about acting is that you get to leave everything about your life behind for a little while. You get to become someone else. Onstage, I don't have to think about the mother who chose drugs over me. I don't have to think about the father I've never known. I don't have to think about how badly I want out of this smothering small town. All I have to think about on that stage is being the best actor I can be.

Because I don't deal with reality all that well, it took me a long time to find the nerve to ask Mirabelle out. Three months, to be exact.

I saw her in the library one day at lunch, and I decided I just needed to do it and get it over with. I asked a friend to get Belle away from her backpack for just a minute by asking her to help him find a book in the shelves. While they were busy, I took her latest fantasy read out of her backpack and taped a dirty picture on the cover with a speech bubble coming out of the dude's mouth: *Can I take you out for breakfast tomorrow morning?*

I hid nearby and watched. When she spotted the picture, she covered her mouth with her hand, and I could tell she was trying so hard not to laugh. She frantically looked around, and when she finally spotted me, she got up, walked over, pulled me into the stacks and gave me the best hug of my life.

"I thought you'd never ask" was her answer to my question. And from that day on, we were just . . . together.

I take a giant swig. Jesus, just make the pain stop. Please.

The past year had been tough on Belle. I get that. And I was as understanding and supportive as I could be. Her little brother, Josh, a freshman, had been diagnosed with leukemia last summer. Josh was being treated at Doernbecher Children's Hospital up in Portland. Her mom and Josh drove the two-hour trip back and forth a lot. Meanwhile, Belle and her dad tried to keep things normal at home, even though there wasn't anything normal about the situation.

But Mr. Starr went to his job every day, doing his electrical work. And Belle went to school, trying her best to keep up her grades. On top of that, she was applying to colleges—although, looking back, I can see how her heart really wasn't in it. I think it was hard for her to think about going away considering everything that was going on with Josh. Like, how could she leave her family when her brother could still be fighting for his life a year from now?

I did everything I could think of to keep her spirits up. She almost didn't audition for *Rabbit Hole,* but I encouraged her to do the play. Told her it would be a good distraction at a time when she really needed it.

She was thrilled when she landed the lead. And in the spring, when she got accepted to four universities, she was happy about that too. But none of that could compare with how she felt when Josh got the good news that he was in remission. On a sunny April day, they invited anyone and everyone to a picnic in the park to celebrate Josh's news. So many people came out to wish them well that day. Afterward, I took her to our favorite twenty-four-hour diner for milkshakes.

"Things are going to be better now, right?" she asked me as she swirled her Oreo milkshake around with the red straw.

I remember looking at her, *really* looking at her, thinking how tired she looked. She couldn't have been sleeping well. Worried sick, just like they say.

I reached over and took her hand. Gave it a squeeze. "Absolutely. He's going to be okay. We'll have a great summer, and then we're outta here. You decided yet?"

"Parker, please don't wait for me," she said. "Go where you want to go."

I'd told her a hundred times already. Still, I told her once more. "Don't you get it? Where you go is the only place I want to be. Do you want to do some research together tomorrow? Try to nail it down?"

"Can't. We're going up to Portland for the day. Gonna do Pip's Doughnuts, OMSI, maybe Powell's."

"With your family, you mean?"

"Yep. Josh's idea. Wants to do a fun Portland trip for a change. See all the good stuff instead of just the inside of a hospital."

"Okay. Well, if you want to do it next week, let me know. We need to decide."

In the end, she decided without me. She chose Southern Oregon University in Ashland. They have a really good marine biology program; plus it's in the same town as the Shakespeare Festival. I can see why she chose it. It suited her.

But the fact that she chose without talking to me about it? That hurt. A lot.

Southern Oregon wasn't even in my top three. For a couple of weeks, I was so torn as to what to do. It felt like she was pulling away from me, like a kite in a windstorm. It was a strange feeling, and I didn't like it.

I ended up choosing University of Oregon in Eugene, about a three-hour drive from Ashland.

"We can still see each other," I told her before school one day. "You know, on weekends."

"Sure," she said. And that was all she'd had to say.

A few weeks later, we were going to prom together.

This was supposed to be one of the best nights of our lives. What a joke.

DOREEN STARR

"Mrs. Starr?"

When I see a uniformed deputy sheriff instead of my daughter standing on the front step, my hand flies to my heart. "Hold on," I tell the deputy. I run back to the bedroom.

As I shimmy out of my pajama bottoms and grab some sweats from the dresser, I say, "Jerry, you need to get up. I think something happened. There's a deputy at the door."

He jumps out of bed and runs to the closet. I throw on a sweatshirt, then grab my phone from the nightstand and text Mirabelle. *Call me, please. Right now.*

Around midnight, I'd drifted off to sleep for a couple of hours. When I woke around two, I turned on my little book light and read a new Louise Penny novel in bed while Jerry slept peacefully beside me. I'd wanted to stay awake until she got home. My girl. The girl who loves sunflowers. The girl who sings Beatles songs every chance she gets. The girl who's always loved an audience and forced us to create the rule "No singing at the dinner table." And the girl who cares deeply about dolphins and killer whales and wants to be a marine biologist someday.

I hadn't stayed awake because I'd been worried about her getting home. No, I trust them. Her and Parker. I'd simply wanted to hear about her evening. She'd texted me that she'd been crowned prom queen. I squealed out loud when I'd read the text. My first thought was maybe this would snap her out of the foul mood she'd been in lately. Of course, given the situation with her brother, I didn't blame her one bit for that. I know it hit her really hard. My second thought was that Parker had probably been crowned king alongside her. But when I asked, she'd told me no, it was some kid named Mario.

Still, I couldn't wait to see her and give her a big hug and hear her describe every little detail. When Parker came to pick her up earlier, I'd told them we expected her home by three at the latest. So when I heard the knock on the door, thirty minutes past her curfew, I actually felt relieved. I figured it was Mirabelle. Thought she must have forgotten her key or something. I swear, both Jerry and Josh could sleep through a fire alarm, so it didn't surprise me I was the only one who heard the knock.

But it isn't my daughter.

I text her again: *I need to know that you're okay.*

Jerry emerges wearing jeans and a plain gray T-shirt. He grabs my hand and we go back to the front door.

"Please, come in," Jerry tells the deputy.

"I'm Deputy Reynolds," he says as he steps through the door. "I'm wondering, is your daughter, Mirabelle, here?"

"No," I say. "She's not home from prom yet. I just texted her. Here, let me try calling her."

I hit Call and put the phone to my ear. It goes straight to voice mail. I call Parker next. But he doesn't pick up either.

"Is there a problem?" Jerry asks the deputy right as I hang up. I go to the front window and pull the curtains back. My stomach lurches when I don't see her car in its normal spot.

"It's gone," I say. "Her car. It isn't here." I look directly at the deputy. "Please, tell us what's going on."

The deputy takes a deep breath before he says, "There's been an accident, but the victim doesn't have any identification on her. The young man who found her says he knows her from school. I'm very sorry, but he says it's Mirabelle."

"A car accident?"

"No, it doesn't appear to have been a car accident. Investigators are on the case. But right now, I need your help. We need to find out for sure if it's your daughter. Do you have some photos you can show me? Preferably from tonight? Before she left the house?"

"Yes," I tell him now, his words buzzing around my head but not quite making sense. "I took some of her and Parker."

"Parker's her boyfriend," Jerry says. "They've been together quite a while. He's a good kid."

"They looked incredible," I say, my hand shaking as I open the photos on my phone. "She was a bundle of nerves today, I assumed it was just pre-prom jitters. When Parker arrived, I thought she might just give us a quick wave and run out the door. But she let me take a few pictures of them, thank goodness. And Jerry, why, he even got her to laugh. Here it is." I hand the deputy my phone. "Isn't it wonderful? It's my favorite."

Jerry had told them that when he went to prom, back in the late eighties, he rented a tux that came with a cane and a top hat.

His grandma had said it looked like he was going onstage to pull a rabbit out of a hat.

Jerry had rolled his eyes at that point. "What was Grandma thinking, saying that? Like I wasn't nervous enough, and now I had to worry that my date might think I looked like Harry Houdini?"

I'd snapped the photo while we all laughed about it. Just like lots of other parents all across this small town would have been doing. Feeling proud. Feeling blessed. I want those feelings back. And I want Mirabelle to walk through that front door.

I watch the deputy's face as he studies the photo. When he looks at me again, he has tears pooling up in his big brown eyes. "Ma'am, does your daughter have a small red birthmark on her right bicep?" he asks.

I try to swallow the lump in my throat. "Yes," I gasp, pain ripping through my body.

Deputy Reynolds looks back and forth between Jerry and me. "I'm so very sorry. Based on that photo, along with the verification of the birthmark, I believe the girl we've found is your daughter. And I'm so sorry to tell you that despite efforts by a deputy on the scene, she has passed away. Of course, we'll need one of you to identify the body to be absolutely certain."

"No," I say. "Oh, no. Please. No." My head drops and tears pour out of me. I feel my knees begin to buckle, but Jerry is right there, holding me up. I feel him sobbing along with me.

"I think we should sit down," the deputy says, motioning toward the sofa. Jerry guides me over.

I don't know how long we cry. Minutes? Hours? The pain is so intense, at times I wonder how it's possible I'm still breathing. At one point, Jerry hands me a handful of tissues.

"You have to tell us what happened," Jerry finally says to the deputy. "Was she walking and got hit by a car? Did someone kidnap her? What in the hell happened?"

"We just don't know enough yet to tell you that. But the area where she was found is being treated as a crime scene. I'm so sorry, but we'll just have to wait and see." He pauses. "Can I get either of you anything? A glass of water, maybe?"

Treated as a crime scene. My baby girl. A crime.

I lean into Jerry. And we both start crying again.

MARIO

t was my first prom. Actually, my first dance. *Ever.* What can I say? I don't have a lot of confidence when it comes to girls.

I'd only ever been on one date and she and I were basically done before we even really got started. Mirabelle and I were paired up as partners in biology and we had a good time in class. She made me laugh. When we had to dissect a worm, I was excited about it. She wasn't. She wanted nothing to do with it. I told her it'd be fun. In the end, she told the teacher she was opposed to hurting animals and that dissecting any creature went against her moral code. She was excused from class that day and given a different assignment to complete.

I thought things between us were fine after that. Like, we were getting along so well while we studied in the library for the final exam that on a whim I asked her if she'd go out with me. Color me shocked when she said yes. We went for pizza and a movie. When I took her home, I walked her to her door. After debating in my head all night whether I should or shouldn't, I decided to kiss her good night. In all honesty, I had no clue what I was doing. She pulled away and said, "Mario. Gross." I told her,

"Sorry," but I didn't want to end on that note, so I leaned in and tried again. But then her dad came outside. As I was kissing her! What the hell? It was so humiliating. It took me two days to get up the nerve to text her.

Her brief reply was like a knife to my already battered ego: *Sorry, I don't think this is going to work out.*

At first, I felt ashamed. Embarrassed. I was afraid she'd tell everyone at school about my piss-poor kissing skills. "He kisses like a reptile with a very active tongue." Or maybe, "Kissing sandpaper would be more fun than kissing that guy." Or simply, "Kissing someone should not be that disgusting."

Yeah, my imagination went into overdrive. But then I got pissed. I mean, come on, she couldn't at least give me one more chance? The anger didn't last long, though. After that, I retreated into myself. I played video games day and night, every spare moment I had. It was the only way I could escape my ugly thoughts. I imagined myself a lonesome loser, unable to get a girlfriend for the rest of my life, all because of one bad kiss.

We got new lab partners the following semester, so I never talked to her again after that. She moved on. Eventually found Parker and they became inseparable. I tried my best to erase the nightmare from my memory.

Until tonight. Prom night. Who could have guessed that the girl I went out with once almost two years ago, Mirabelle Starr, would be crowned prom queen while I was crowned prom king alongside her?

When we both went up onstage, she hugged me, and all the humiliation and awkwardness I'd felt that night on her porch came rushing back. Besides, the last thing I wanted was to be prom king. Maybe some people like that kind of attention, but I'm not some people.

And then the crown. How did he not see it? How did the principal not notice that there were worms crawling on the velvet fabric? It was terrible. Like a tame version of the movie *Carrie*.

The worst part? After the administrators got rid of the worms and calmed me down, they had no idea what to do. They put the crown back on my head and said we just needed to carry on. And so it was time for our dance.

It was probably the longest three minutes of my life. Everyone was watching us. Everyone. The spotlight shined on us and we didn't say one word to each other. Not. One. Part of me wanted to tell her off since I was ninety-five percent sure she was responsible for the prank because of our history together in biology. But I didn't have proof. And maybe it was just a weird coincidence that the prankster chose worms instead of beetles or centipedes or whatever. I mean, if it was her, how did she know I was going to be the winner? Unless she campaigned for me to win or stuffed the ballot box or something.

As if that weren't bad enough, she had to go tweet that stuff to Elana about keeping her mouth closed if she kissed me. In the span of, like, thirty minutes, I experienced more humiliation than I had in my entire eighteen years of life.

I didn't even want to go to prom. But a couple of things happened that made it hard to say no. The senior class elected me Prince of Intellect, and the expectation is that all the princes and princesses will be at prom. I could have gone alone, but then my mother asked if I might take Elana as a favor to her dad. See, my mom's been the office manager for Dr. Dexter, a dentist, for a really long time. He's Elana's father, and apparently, he really wanted her to go. The girl has had a tough time of it since her mom ran off with another guy without saying a word to her family before she left. Like, not even a goodbye note. What kind of monster does that?

My mom did her best to support them after it happened, so I heard about Elana sometimes. I never paid much attention to her before, but since her mom left, I've noticed how much of a loner Elana is at school. Like, even more than me. I'll admit, I felt sorry for her.

Anyway, Mom kept bugging me about taking her. She said I'd be doing her a huge favor because Dr. Dexter was tied up in knots about his little girl. He told my mom Elana was really down and struggling, and therapy didn't seem to be helping. Said she needed someone to make her feel special and cared for, even if it was for only one night. Of course, that didn't sound right at all to me. A night with me would fix what therapy couldn't? Yeah, sure.

So although I felt bad for the girl, it was a hard no from me at first. I was fine going alone.

"Mario, I really think you'll have a lot more fun if you have a date," Mom argued a few weeks ago while we ate burgers she'd gotten from the Hasty Freeze. "It's just one night. You'd be doing such a nice thing for the girl. Don't you think you'll be bored if you go alone?"

"Um . . . no?"

"How about if I buy you some nice rims for your truck once you get it?"

Now she had my attention. "Wait. Really?"

"Yes. Really."

I thought it'd be worth it. God, I wish I could go back. I shouldn't have let my mom sway me like that. It was a mistake. *Such* a mistake.

ELANA

Oh, Mario. Prom night started out so well, too.

He picked me up and had a gorgeous wrist corsage that consisted of a single white orchid. So simple. So stunning. It left me speechless, and trust me, that's not something that happens very often.

"Do you like it?" he asked me after I'd stared at it far too long.

"Yes. It's really pretty."

"Oh, good. I was worried for a second."

I ran my hand down the flared skirt of my short, sparkly dress, wondering if he'd say something. I loved my dress so much—it was everything I'd wanted it to be. It cost Daddy a fortune, but he hadn't even blinked when I'd showed him the price tag. I think he felt a little guilty that I had to shop with him instead of with a mother, like most girls. It's been almost a year since she left. I go weeks now without crying, but god, do I still miss her.

After I kissed my dad goodbye, I grabbed my silver wrap and my little black handbag and walked out to the truck with Mario. Not the most luxurious ride for the prom, but oh well. When I got in, I caught a whiff of lemon. Like Pledge furniture polish or something. I imagined him looking in the cupboard for something to use to clean his dash and thinking, *Hey, maybe this will work*. All for me. The thought made me smile, because if he did do that, it meant he cared what I thought of him.

Mario had asked me to the prom just two weeks ago, shortly after he'd been named Prince of Intellect. I had tried to put the dance out of my mind. No one had asked, and so I figured I'd be stuck at home in my yoga pants watching Netflix while everyone else in my class was out having fun. When Mario came to my locker before school and asked if I'd go with him, I wasn't sure I'd heard him right at first.

"What'd you say?" I'd asked him.

"I was wondering if you'd go to prom with me," he said again.

A couple of things. First, I barely knew who the guy was. Okay, yes, his mom works for my dad. But it's not like the two of us hang out at my dad's dental practice after school. The only time you'll find me there is when it's time to get my teeth cleaned. And even though Mario had been in a few of my classes over the years, I don't think I'd ever spoken to him. Second, I'd resigned myself to the fact that I wouldn't be going. The dance was only two weeks away! Everyone else had their dates figured out weeks, even months, before. So when he asked, to say I was surprised is an understatement.

"Mario," I replied. "Are you serious right now?"

His eyes narrowed but he didn't get upset. All he said was "A hundred percent. I mean, I heard you don't have a date yet, so I thought—"

"I'd go with you?" I asked. As soon as I said it, I realized I sounded like a total bitch. "Sorry. I didn't mean . . . I just . . . ."

I looked around, wondering if everyone was watching us. Judging us. But no one seemed to care.

I shrugged. "Sure. Why not? It's the only senior prom we'll ever have, yeah?"

He smiled. He's kind of cute when he smiles. Although I couldn't help but think he really needed a haircut.

"Here," he said. "Let me give you my number. If you could let me know the color of your dress, my mom says it's important that we coordinate. Although hopefully she's not expecting me to get a matching dress."

"You could always just go with black and white," I told him.

"But no horizontal stripes because they'll make me look fat?"

I smiled. "You're funny. I'm just saying, you can't go wrong with a classic."

"I've always wanted to be called classy."

"Well, here's your chance."

We exchanged numbers and the bell rang. He started to take off and then turned around and said, "So you'll text me? There might be other reasons we need to know your colors. Sorry, Elana. Not really an expert with these things. Shocking, I know."

"No problem," I told him. "It's all good."

For two weeks, I've been wondering why he asked me of all people to the prom. Me, the weird loner girl. The one everyone at school loves to hate. An easy target, my dad said once, to make themselves feel better about their own miserable lives.

But if Mario cleaned his truck for me, then it seemed to me like maybe he actually cared. And god, suddenly I was actually excited about going to prom with him.

MARIO

The Dexters live in one of the nicest houses in town. It's one of those Tudor-style homes with a steeply pitched roof. Lots of gorgeous brick. And their yard? Immaculate. Guessing Mr. Dexter hires someone to do it for him. Some parts of town, people just let their yards go. Mom looks on the bright side and says it's not a bad thing, since clovers and dandelions make the bees happy. Of course, the yards full of junk are a whole other matter. Don't think anyone's happy with those. Sometimes I wonder why someone like Mr. Dexter stays in a town like this. Probably scared a big city would chew his daughter up and spit her out.

When Elana came to the front door, she looked good. Like, *amazing*. It took every bit of courage I had not to hightail it out of there because there was no way I could be good enough for her. She should have been walking the red carpet in Hollywood instead of a dingy brown carpet in the Elks Lodge.

I'm guessing she'd spent hours curling her long brown hair, plus she had glittery eye shadow on her eyelids and wore dark red lipstick. Seriously, the girl was drop-dead gorgeous, and maybe I should have been patting myself on the back for being the chosen one, but that is not at all what I was doing.

No, instead I stood there wondering why this girl was such a loner and why no one else had asked her to the dance. It didn't make sense. Was this some huge prank my mother was in on? Except what kind of mother would do that? It was like there was something missing from the equation. Something I didn't know. And I can't deny I had a funny feeling about it for a quick second.

But all my anxiety, or whatever it was, went away when her dad came to the door and shook my hand. He looked so happy. And maybe, I decided, if he didn't have a care in the world about us going to prom together, I shouldn't either.

"You kids have fun, all right?" he said. "Elana, how about two o'clock for a curfew? That should be late enough, don't you think?"

"Yep," she said before she leaned up and kissed him on the cheek. "Please don't worry."

And that was that.

When she slid onto the seat of my truck, she turned and gave me a big smile as I closed the passenger door. I went around and hopped in from my side.

"Your truck smells good," she said. "Lemony."

"Thanks. I was worried it might smell like French fries or some shit, so I gave it a good cleaning."

"You go off campus for lunch, usually?"

"Yeah. Me and Lucas. What about you?"

While she told me how she usually ate in one of the big, comfy chairs in the commons, I started up the truck and backed out of her driveway.

"So where are we going first?" she asked.

"My house. For just a few minutes. If that's okay? My mom is dying for some photos. Sorry."

"Don't apologize," she said. "It's fine." She paused. "So your dad won't be there?"

It seemed like she was fishing for information about my family. Maybe I should have been bothered by it, but I wasn't. I knew about her mother, so it seemed only fair she should know something about my situation.

"All I know about my dad is that he lives in Chile. My mom met him while vacationing there with a friend. She came home, found out she was pregnant, and never told him about me."

"Wow. Do you know anything about him?"

"Only his name. Mario Garcia."

"Aw, so she named you after him. That's sweet. But don't you want to know more? Aren't you curious?"

"Yeah. I am. Someday I want to go there and try to find him. Not sure my mom will be happy about that, but it's my dad, you know?"

"Yeah. I get it."

I decide it's time to lighten the mood. "So you probably noticed my mom didn't make me get a matching dress. Hope you're not disappointed."

She smiled. "I did notice. And you really *do* look classy in black and white."

I knew this was where I should tell her she looked nice. I hadn't done that yet. But I was so nervous I'd screw it up. Saying "You look nice" sounded so lame in my mind. Like, in the compliment department, *nice* is a pair of flannel pajamas. If I said, "You look smoking hot," I'd probably sound like a horny asshole. *Gorgeous* or *beautiful* sounded like words only a boyfriend should say. So, in typical Mario fashion, I said nothing. Better to be safe than say the wrong thing, that's my introverted motto.

She pulled her phone out of her little black bag. "Dad says 'Please no drinking and driving.' God. Like a quick text from him is going to keep you from doing it? Why do parents have to be so annoying, anyway?"

"I think maybe . . . it's their job?"

She smiled. "I guess you're right."

"For what it's worth, my mom really likes working for your dad. Says he's a good guy. Which makes me happy because I wouldn't really want my mom working for a jerk."

"He's all right, I guess. Most of the time. And just so you know, I adore your mom. She was so nice to us after . . . well, you know."

No way was I gonna talk about that. "She's beyond excited we're going to prom together. Not sure if I should tell you this or not, but this is only the second time I've ever been out with a girl. So be prepared for about three hundred photos."

"Who was the first girl?" she asks.

"Mirabelle Starr."

"Oh, really?"

"Yeah. It didn't last long, though."

"So, Mario. Can I ask you a question?"

I shrugged. "Sure."

"Did my dad put you up to this somehow?"

"What do you mean?" I asked as I got a sinking feeling in my stomach. It hadn't occurred to me that she might want to know how we ended up here. That it would matter to her if I asked her to prom because I wanted to rather than someone telling me I should. But of course it would matter.

"It's just strange," she said. "We hardly know each other. Why'd you ask me?"

"How about because I wanted to?"

"Not buying it. I bet my dad asked your mom for a favor. Didn't he?"

I didn't know what to say next. If I told the truth, she might get pissed and refuse to talk to me the rest of the night. Not exactly the way I wanted to spend my one and only prom. On the other hand, if I lied and she found out at some point, that would be bad too.

"Okay, here's the deal: My mom suggested it. And I liked the idea. So I asked you."

"But you weren't forced to ask me?"

I laughed. "Elana. Did you see anyone putting a gun to my head that day at your locker?"

I looked over at her and she was smiling. "No. I didn't." The smile disappeared. "But you know what I mean. Parents can be very, um, influential, if they want to be."

The longer we talked, the more I was one hundred percent certain that a little white lie was absolutely appropriate here. "Well, in this case, the most influential person was me. Okay?"

When I glanced over at her again, she seemed to have relaxed a bit more into the seat. It felt like I'd said exactly the right thing.

Until I heard her say, in a very firm voice, "I just hope I don't find out that you're lying to me."

So let me ask you: What would *you* have done?

You would have lied even harder. Just like I did. "My mom suggested it. That's all. I swear."

JANICE WOODS

When Mario and Elana pulled into the driveway, I opened the door and hurried outside. I couldn't help it, I was just so excited. This year *I* was going to be one of those moms posting prom pictures on social media. I honestly didn't think I'd ever get the chance.

Mario's a quiet kid. He has friends, sure, but he's a homebody. As a mother, I worry a lot about my son. I was really outgoing in high school, so it's hard not to wonder if he feels like he's missing out on stuff. It's gotta be tough on a kid's ego if you're not one of the popular guys. Maybe I should have pushed him more when it came to sports. He played soccer when he was younger, but then when he hit middle school, he stopped. Said he didn't feel like he was talented enough to play anymore. Oh, how I wanted to change that. Change his views of himself. But there's only so much a mother can do.

He puts in a lot of effort at school. Gets good grades. Works part-time and hangs out with Lucas, his best friend, when he has some downtime. He seems mostly happy, and maybe that's all that really matters.

When I saw that truck with a lovely girl sitting next to Mario, my heart fluttered. I thought maybe it would be the start of better things for my son. I hoped his last few weeks of senior year would be filled with a nice girl, good friends and fun times.

"Hello, Elana," I said when she stepped out. "You look stunning."

We'd rented Mario an ordinary black-and-white tux. The salesman tried to talk us into going with something a bit unconventional, but Mario liked the tried-and-true classic the best. When I saw how Elana looked, I realized we'd done the right thing, because who was going to notice what he was wearing next to her?

"Hello, Ms. Woods," she said with a bit of a pinched smile.

I looked over at Mario and he was giving me a panicked twirl of his finger, as if to say "Hurry it up."

"If you could go up to the front porch, I'll get a few photos real quick," I told them. "Won't take long at all, I promise."

"Take all the time you want," Elana said as she climbed the steps. She looked like a model, her silver dress so pretty against the backdrop of our little blue bungalow. "Even though he's tried to convince me otherwise, I'm not sure Mario is all that excited about going."

For a moment, I was speechless. Why would she say such a thing? It upset me. Finally, I said, "What are you talking about? Of course he's excited. It's his prom. And yours too. The two of you are going to have a wonderful time."

Mario glanced at me and I could see all the color had drained from his face. Had she discovered I'd put him up to this? But how? Mario wouldn't have mentioned it, I was sure of that. And it

38

didn't seem to me like her dad would say anything either. Maybe she'd just made a wild guess. Well, I wasn't going to play into it. Besides, whatever had transpired, Mario was a nice boy and he'd do his best to make sure she'd have a good time.

"How should we stand, Mom?" Mario asked. He seemed to be doing his best to keep us on task.

"Elana, if you could lean up against the post, and, Mario, why don't you stand next to her." As they moved into position, I watched them. She appeared to be guarded. Like she couldn't figure out if she should allow herself to relax and have fun. I racked my brain, trying to figure out if there was anything I could do to help the situation. But I couldn't think of a thing. So I took some photos and sent them on their way. Elana didn't say another word, but oh, her eyes. They told me everything her mouth didn't.

I thought of my son and how up until that night, he'd had to deal with very little real drama. I'd worked hard at giving him a nice, normal life—just me and him. Sure, there were times when it would have been nice having his father around. But I never mentioned him. My goal for us had always been to simply be happy. What if Elana decided to make the next five to six hours agonizing for Mario? Decided to make him feel bad for trying to be a nice guy?

I told myself it was only one night. Whatever happened, he could put up with anything for one night.

MARIO

"Mario, I'm Detective Green. I know the deputy took your statement earlier, but I have a few more questions I'd like to ask you."

He's sitting across from me, in the backseat of the patrol car. It's been what feels like hours, and they still haven't let me go. It's so stuffy in here, like I'm in a sauna. I want to ask if he'd mind opening a window, but I'm guessing the answer would be no. I tell myself to just stay calm and answer his questions as quickly and politely as possible. I can get some air and a drink of water in a few minutes.

"Sure, go ahead. Is someone else going to talk to Elana?"

"Yes. We're talking to her too, don't worry. So, can you tell me what you were doing all the way out here, exactly?"

"We went to a party nearby. At Jason's house. He's got a big farmhouse on a lot of land, so his parents said he could have people over after prom. It kind of got out of hand, but anyway . . ."

"Who's 'we'?"

"Me and Elana. A bunch of other kids were there from school too, though. Obviously."

"Where were you before the party?"

"We went out to dinner. Then the dance."

"What time did you leave the party?"

"I don't know. Wasn't paying attention."

"Did you see the deceased, Miss Mirabelle Starr, at the party?"

I gulp. "Yes. She was there."

"Did you speak to her?"

"It was a party. I talked to a lot of people."

"Okay. So what did you say to Mirabelle?"

"I don't remember." I don't want to lie. But I don't want to tell him what was said. At this point, it's not important anyway.

"Was anyone else around who might have witnessed the conversation?"

It's hard to hide my frustration with these questions. "I don't know, man. Look, have you ever been to a party? Do you even know what it's like? People everywhere. Music playing. Couples making out in bedrooms. Arguments outside. There were a lot of people there. If you want to know if I threatened to kill her or something like that, the answer is no. I'd never hurt her. I'd never hurt anyone. I swear."

He stares at me. "You're getting awfully defensive. I didn't ask if you threatened to kill her. I just want to know what you talked about."

"Like I said, I don't remember."

"Did you know her prior to tonight?"

"Yes."

"How well?"

"What do you mean?"

"How well did you know her? Friend? Acquaintance? Ex-girlfriend?"

"I, um, I went out with her once. But it was just one date. A couple of years ago."

He scribbles in his notebook.

"How have things been between the two of you since?"

I briefly consider telling him about what happened earlier. With the crown. But it all seems so petty now. It was a stupid joke, that's all.

"Fine, I guess. Hardly ever talk to her, to be honest."

"Okay. So you're driving out here on Wessinger Road after the party. Where were you going?"

"Uh, I was just gonna drive around for a while. Until Elana, um, felt better. You know."

"Did you provide her with the alcohol?"

"No, I didn't. And look, I realize now that I should have been paying more attention to how much she was drinking. I feel really bad that she got so drunk so fast. She was my date and under my care." I rub my eyes for a second. God, this is such a nightmare.

"All right. You're driving around because she was intoxicated. And then what happened?"

"I saw something. In the ditch. And what I saw, it freaked me out because it looked like a body. I stopped. Got out of my truck. Used the flashlight on my phone to see better. And that's when the deputy pulled up."

"When did you realize it was Mirabelle?"

"I could see her face pretty well with my flashlight."

"How long were you standing there, would you say?"

"Not long. A minute, maybe?"

"And yet you didn't run down into the ditch to check on the girl right away? How come?"

"I was going to," I try to explain. "You gotta understand, it all happened so fast and I was scared of what it would look like if someone came along. And then, you know, the cop did show up and I figured it was better that a professional go down and check on her."

"Hm." He points to my hands. "What's the dirt under your fingernails from?"

Instinctively, I ball them up. "I, uh . . . was messing around at the party. In the backyard. With some of the guys."

"Messing around how, exactly?"

"Someone tackled me. Then others joined in. They were giving me a hard time because I was prom king."

He's jotting stuff down. Finally, he says, "All right. You stay here. I need to check on a couple of things."

"Yeah. Okay."

A little while later, one of the other patrol cars takes off. I'm pretty sure it's the one with Elana in it. I kind of figure they got all the information they need and they'll let me go. But that's not what happens. Deputy Mitchell opens the door and says, "Mario, I need you to step out of the car, please."

So I do.

He pulls out handcuffs and locks one into place on my wrist before bringing it behind my back. "Mario Woods, you're under arrest for contributing to the delinquency of a minor and possession of an open container. You have the right to remain silent. Anything you say can and will be used against you in a court of law. You have the right to an attorney. If you cannot afford an attorney, one will be provided for you. Do you understand these rights?"

"Open container? What are you talking about?"

"Your girlfriend had an open bottle in her purse," the deputy says.

"She's not my girlfriend. And what about her? What happens to Elana? Are you arresting her too?"

No one answers me. I can't believe this is happening. Why am I the one under arrest when Elana is the one who's been drinking?

The deputy helps me into the backseat. "Can I at least make a phone call?" I ask. "My mom is going to be wondering what's happened when I don't come home."

"Once we get you booked, you'll have access to a phone. You can call her then."

This is insane. How is this even fair? I was doing my best to get Elana home safely, without her dad, or anyone else, ever knowing what happened. And now I'm being arrested?

Something isn't right. Like, this shouldn't be happening. They should give me a warning or a ticket and send me home. Shouldn't they? Why do they think I belong in jail?

Whatever it is, whatever's going on, right now my hands are tied. Literally.

ELANA

After we left the amateur photo shoot at Mario's house, Mario told me we were going to the Steak House. It's definitely the nicest restaurant in town (and not even that nice compared to big-city restaurants) and I imagined that it would be crazy-busy on prom night. I tried to put my dad and Mario's mom out of my mind. Maybe they did put Mario up to it, but at this point, what could I do about it? I didn't want to be pissed the entire night. First of all, it wasn't fair to Mario, and second of all, it wasn't fair to me.

He didn't say much on the way to the restaurant, so it gave me time to cool off. I liked that about him—that he gave me some space when I obviously needed it.

"You made reservations, right?" I asked when he pulled into the parking lot.

"Um . . ."

I looked at him. "No way. Please tell me you're joking."

He shrugged. "I didn't think of it. They gotta save some seats for walk-ins, yeah? I think it'll be fine."

He cleaned his truck but he didn't think about making

reservations? My stomach grumbled. I'd hardly eaten anything all day. If they couldn't make room for us, what would we do? Head to the Hasty Freeze drive-through?

I waited as Mario came around to my side of the truck and opened the door for me. He helped me out and I said, "Thanks."

There were a few other couples getting out of their cars. All of them looked at us as we walked across that parking lot. Some of them whispered to each other. Whatever. It's not like I wasn't used to that kind of shit.

"You all right?" Mario asked.

"Fine."

"You sure? Because you seem a little salty." He winked at me. A cute wink, I had to admit. And then, in a really soft voice, he said, "They're just jealous, that's all. You're drop-dead gorgeous and they can't stand it."

You know what makes Mario different? When he says stuff like that, he sounds completely sincere. Like he really means it. It made me smile.

Okay, so maybe his mom twisted his arm to ask me to prom. And maybe he was a noob at this whole going-out thing. But the guy was nice. And I figured that should definitely count for something.

The hostess immediately asked us if we had a reservation.

"I didn't think of it," Mario said. "I'm sorry. I hope that doesn't mean we can't get a table."

I almost told him this was where he should slip her some cash. I'd seen it on TV once or twice. But what if he didn't have a lot of cash on him? And maybe that only worked in Hollywood, not in small-town Oregon.

The hostess studied the computer screen in front of her. "You know, we've had one no-show in the past thirty minutes, so I can put you there."

When he looked at me as the hostess grabbed our menus, I told him, "Looks like this is your lucky night." As soon as I said it, I realized how it sounded. I braced myself for some gross comeback about how he hoped I was right. But that isn't what I got. Instead, he said, "You said yes two weeks ago when I asked you. Seems like that's when my lucky streak began, don't you think?"

So much for a lucky streak.

Now I'm sitting in this room with a short, pudgy bald guy with a mustache that desperately needs to be trimmed. Ugh, I hate facial hair. Disgusting.

"Elana, I'm Detective Bellinger. I'm just going to make sure I have all the information we need before we release you to a parent, okay?"

"Look, I've been sitting here for a really long time. I want to go home."

"I know. I'm sorry. We had to finish up our investigation at the scene. You'll be out of here soon."

"Okay. Then ask."

"Did Mario give you the alcohol?"

"No. I don't know who gave it to me. I don't remember. I already gave the deputy what I had on me. It wasn't much."

"Any idea how long you were out of it?"

"I don't really know."

"You didn't see anything unusual? Hear anything?"

I shake my head. Hard. "No. Nothing." I pause. "Where's Mario?"

"That's none of your concern right now. You need to tell me what happened. In your own words. Why don't we start at the beginning? Where'd you go first last night?"

"To dinner at the Steak House. And after that, we went to the dance. It was held at the Elks Lodge, but you probably already know that."

"How long did you stay there?"

"We left around ten-thirty. Right after they crowned Mario prom king."

"Hmm. And were you the queen?"

"No. That was Mirabelle."

He scrunches up his face a little at that. "Mirabelle? As in, the girl we just found in the ditch?"

"Yes."

"Huh. Anything happen between them? Mario and Mirabelle? That you know of?"

"Well, they were prom king and queen tonight, and someone put worms in Mario's crown. Mario made a comment when we left that he thought she may have been behind it. Super juvenile, if you ask me."

"He specifically said he thought Mirabelle did it?"

"Yeah."

"Why'd he think that?"

"I don't know, he didn't really say. There were also some things

48

she said on Twitter that weren't very nice. But then, she's never been a very nice girl."

He tilts his head slightly and his eyes narrow. "What do you mean?"

"She likes to mess with people. She thinks it's funny, but it's not."

"Did Mario seem angry with her?"

"I don't know if *angry* is the right word. Mostly he seemed really humiliated by the whole thing. I felt bad for him."

"How long have you known Mario?"

"Since middle school, I guess. Never talked to him much, though."

"How'd you end up going to prom with him?"

"He was the only one who asked me."

"All right. So after you left the dance, where'd you go?"

"To the party at Jason's house."

"Did you speak to Mirabelle while you were there?"

"Nope. Why would I? She was with her boyfriend, Parker. Most of the time, anyway. You going to talk to him too?"

"Yes. We'll be talking to a lot of people. What about Mario and Mirabelle? Did they talk to each other?"

"Yeah. She asked if she could speak to him alone. He told me later that she wanted to apologize. Clear the air. Whatever."

"Did you believe him?"

"Of course. Why would he lie about something like that? Hey, I'm curious: Is this the first murder in Willow? I've been wondering about that. A small town like ours, things like this just don't happen. Do they?"

"Let's stick to the task at hand, shall we?"

I lean back in the chair and close my eyes. Bend my head left and right, because my neck and shoulders are killing me.

"I'm so tired," I tell him. "I don't know if I can do this anymore."

"Do you drink coffee?" he asks.

"No. Only tea."

He stands up. "Let me get you some. Maybe a glass of water too, huh? It's important we finish this, Elana. A girl is dead. You get that, right?"

"Believe me. I get it."

"I'll be right back."

I drop my head on the desk and close my eyes. All I want to do is sleep. Forget all this bullshit and lose myself to a place where only dreams exist.

JERRY STARR

The medical examiner has a small office in the basement of the courthouse. I go around to the back of the building, as I've been instructed, and knock on the door. It's Sunday, after all, so the courthouse is closed today. A moment later, a man opens the door. An older man with thin gray hair, thick glasses, and kind brown eyes.

"Mr. Starr?"

"Yes."

"Hello. Please come in. I'm Dr. Jenson." I've barely stepped through the door when he asks, "Can I get you anything to drink? A glass of water, perhaps?"

"No, I'm fine, thank you."

"I want you to know I'm very sorry for your loss. I know this is a difficult time. I'll do my best to make this as easy as possible. Please take a seat there."

He points to a chair across from a cluttered desk. While I take a seat, he moves files and paperwork, trying to create a clear space to work. He says softly, "As you know, your visit here is twofold. I need you to officially identify the body. And then I'll have some forms for you to fill out. Because of the nature of the death, we need to perform an autopsy. This is not optional. Once that's finished, her body can be released to the funeral home."

"Okay."

"All right. Let's complete the identification process. I know this is going to be difficult for you. I'm going to show you two photos, and I'll describe everything that you're going to see as best I can before I turn over the photos. Are you ready to begin?"

I don't want to say yes. But what choice do I have? This is what I'm here to do. And no one else can do it for me. "Yes. I'm ready."

"The first one is a photo of her body from the neck down. You'll see some marks on her neck but try your best not to focus on those. It's the clothes we want to show you, since she still has her clothes on from last night. Are you ready?"

I nod.

He pushes the photo, facedown, across the table. And then he turns it over. The first thing I see are the marks, but I force my eyes to move away from them. I see the pretty red dress. The strappy heels. Her hands with her freshly painted nails. The ruby ring we gave her for her sixteenth birthday. You think you're ready for it, you know? You think you've done everything you can to prepare yourself, but there's still a part of you that hopes they're wrong.

"That's her," I say in a whisper.

"This next one is of her face. She looks peaceful. Like she's sleeping. Okay?"

I take a deep breath and nod again. When he turns it over, I can't keep the emotions in check any longer. The sobs come hard and fast.

It's her. Our Mirabelle. No question.

"Is this your daughter?" he asks me softly.

I can barely get the word out. "Yes."

I think of her in a cold room somewhere, lying on a table, and I can hardly bear the thought. It hurts so much to think of her like that. Damn it all to hell.

As I wipe my face with a handkerchief, I say, "I don't understand how a girl winds up in a ditch on prom night with no car in sight. Do you have any information yet about how she died? Do you know if she suffered? Was there any sign of . . ." I can't even finish the sentence.

"I can tell you that it appears to be strangulation. The state forensic pathologist will be arriving to do the autopsy this afternoon. I'm hoping that we'll have more details to share with you by tomorrow. Of course, sometimes things happen. Other cases require attention. But please know, we'll do everything we can to finish our report as quickly as possible."

He reaches over and gets a clipboard with some papers on it along with a black pen. "Again, Mr. Starr, I'm sorry for your loss."

Words I never thought I'd hear in relation to my eighteen-year-old daughter.

MARIO

keep wondering what Elana's told them. It's making my stomach hurt. What if she said something that makes me look even worse than I already do? She could so easily do that.

All night, I tried to be a gentleman. I tried to make sure she had a good time. But honestly, I don't know what she thinks of me. I don't know if she likes me or hates me. Who knows, maybe it'd make her really happy to see them lock me up in jail and throw away the key.

Did she tell them the truth? A version of the truth? Or some bold made-up lie that will basically blindside me? Again, I don't know. And that not knowing is killing me right now.

When we get to the jail, Deputy Mitchell has me stand on a black rubber mat and hand over all my personal belongings. He takes my wallet, my keys, my belt, and my phone. Even takes my shoelaces out of my shoes. Has me sign a form that lists everything I had on me. Then he searches me from head to toe. Literally. Every pocket is gone through and I have to take off my socks and turn them inside out to make sure I'm not hiding something there.

After that, he takes me inside and I'm placed in a holding cell with a bunch of other dudes. Some are sitting on benches. Some are sitting on the floor. A couple are even lying on the floor. There's one phone on the wall and a line to use it.

"We'll call your name when we're ready to process you," the deputy says. "In the meantime, think of this like the DMV. It's crowded, people are in a lousy mood, and you wait in line a lot."

"Great," I say, my voice loaded with sarcasm. "How long am I going to be here?"

"It'll be a while to get you processed. After that, you'll go in a holding cell until your court appearance tomorrow."

Tomorrow? I have to stay the night in this place? I don't belong here. I really, really don't. My heart's racing and I feel dizzy. God, is this what a panic attack feels like?

I imagine my mom telling me to breathe.

Breathe, Mario. Just breathe. Nice and slow.

Once I've calmed myself down, I decide there's nothing to do but get in line for the phone. As I wait, I try to figure out how to break this ugly news to my poor mother. She's gotta be worried sick. Probably hasn't slept a wink since I last called her.

The guy in line in front of me turns around. He's got a shaved head and is wearing a T-shirt that says *Jenius* on it. One of his arms is covered with a colorful tattoo that makes it look like he's got a machine for an arm. It's wild. While he eyes my tux, he says, "Must have been some prom night, huh?"

I don't want to talk to the guy. I don't want to talk to anyone.

Luckily, before I can answer, someone yells to the dude on the phone, "Come on, man. Time is up!"

Others start yelling at him. Cussing at him. Jenius turns back around and yells profanities along with the rest of them.

And so it goes. At least an hour later, it's my turn.

"Hello?"

"Mom? Can you hear me?"

"Mario? What's going on? I've been trying to call you. Where are you?"

"I know. I'm sorry. They've arrested me."

"Oh, dear god. What on earth for?"

"Elana was drunk. Had something in her purse, too. Since she's a minor, I'm in a lot of trouble, I guess."

"So are you saying you're in jail?"

"They're in the process of booking me now. The deputy says when he's finished, I'll be held here until I can see a judge sometime on Monday."

I can tell she's trying to stay calm, but her voice is shaking. "Oh, Mario, this is terrible. What can I do? Should I get you a lawyer?"

I think of how hard she works. How she's been saving her money for years to take a vacation to Greece. She's dreamed of going there for as long as I can remember. She even has an entire Pinterest board devoted to it. Now she has to hire someone to help me with this mess? Before I can even answer, she says, "Never mind. The answer to that question is a definite yes. You found a dead body. There might be more to your arrest than they're letting on. I'll find someone as soon as possible. Hang in there, honey. It's only a couple of days, right? I wonder if you get a cell by yourself or . . . ?"

Her voice trails off. I hadn't even thought of that—that I might have to share a cell with other suspected criminals.

Cell. Criminal. Court appearance.

Somehow, I went to prom and ended up in hell.

ELANA

For some reason, in this small, ugly room at the police station, I can't stop thinking about my mom.

In fifth or sixth grade, Mom declared that every Tuesday night would be girls' night. She and I would go out to dinner, or catch a movie, or stay home and watch YouTube makeup tutorials and try them out. I can remember watching her carefully apply three different colors of eye shadow and being so amazed at how perfect it came out. I rarely got the results I wanted. It often looked really fake on me. Ugly and fake.

"Keep practicing," she told me once when I was especially frustrated. "Remember, I've been doing this a lot longer than you have. Besides, you don't need much, with your beautiful skin and pretty features."

She always looked so polished. Like she knew exactly what she was doing and no one better get in her way. I swear, even running to the grocery store to pick up a couple of things, she looked like she was on her way to have drinks with A-listers in Hollywood.

I couldn't help it—I constantly compared myself to her.

In middle school, when everything started to go downhill for me, I so often wished I could *be* her. Boys would jeer as I walked by because of my developing breasts (that were a lot larger than I wanted them to be), and I wouldn't say a word. Nicole, my best friend since kindergarten, would tell them to knock it off or shut up or go throw themselves into the river.

"Why do you take that?" Nicole asked me after an especially difficult day in eighth grade, when I'd worn a sweater that had become a little too small.

I didn't have an answer for her. Deep down, maybe I thought I deserved it.

And I never told my mother about what was happening because I worried she'd be disappointed in me.

Nicole was such a good friend to me. It devastated me when her dad got transferred to Boston right before the start of our freshman year. We'd taken ballet together for a couple years in elementary school. Played the flute together in middle school. Besides my mom, she was the one friend I could count on.

After Nicole left, Mom kept telling me I'd make new friends. She had no idea what middle school had been like for me. I pretty much hated everyone and trusted no one. But she never knew that.

Eventually, I got tired of her questions and started lying to make them stop. Told her I'd met a couple of girls and we ate lunch together every day. With each year that passed, the lies got better and better. As far as my parents were concerned, I had friends and I was happy. Never mind that I was home every weekend. Never mind that I wasn't involved in sports or other extracurricular activities. My grades were good, and I said I had friends, so they believed me.

Or they didn't want to deal with the truth.

And then, out of the blue, Mom decided to start looking for work, even though Dad told her we were doing just fine on his salary. It wasn't about the money, she said. Next thing we knew, she'd gotten a job as a receptionist at an emergency vet hospital. She worked strange hours, slept a lot when she was home, and it wasn't long before girls' night went by the wayside.

I've never asked my father, though I've wanted to, if he suspected anything. Sometimes I think back and wonder how I didn't see it. How I didn't see her slipping away from us, little by little, each day.

One day last July, she went to work and never came home. When Dad called the vet's office, they told him they hadn't seen her for weeks. She'd quit and never told us. She and her new guy had probably been planning their escape for months.

Dad had his office staff cancel all his appointments. He drove around town, trying to figure out what happened. When a patient of his who works at the Rite-Aid told him she'd seen Mom with a man she didn't recognize, stocking up on snacks and magazines, he realized life as we knew it was over.

"Maybe she just needs a break," I'd told him. "Maybe she'll be back."

He bit his lip as tears welled up in his eyes. Finally, he said, "I think that's wishful thinking, sweetheart. Just please know that I love you and I'm here for you. Okay?"

Except he wasn't there for me. Not in the way that I needed, anyway.

Meanwhile, I held out hope for a couple of weeks. And then, one day I woke up and I realized he was right. She was gone and she wasn't coming back. That afternoon, I put on my suit and went to the pool, hoping to swim until I was so tired, I couldn't think straight. Because I was tired of thinking and worrying and wondering.

A group of kids from school were there and I should have listened to my gut and turned around and gone home. Instead, I waved and smiled and jumped right in to join them as if I belonged there. This was my chance, I thought. My chance to change things. To try to make senior year better than the last three years. Maybe I'd finally manage to make friends who cared about me; friends who'd let me cry on their shoulders and vice versa. I wanted that almost as much as I wanted my mom to come back.

But they had different plans for me. Someone had an underwater GoPro. And someone took photos of my bottom half without me knowing it. Unflattering photos. And by the time I'd gotten home, they were all over social media.

Sometimes I wonder: If my mom had been around, would I have told her what happened? Or would I have continued with my lies to make her happy? I realized a while ago that's what I'd always been trying to do—make her happy. And I'd failed.

Once in a while, if I close my eyes tight, I can imagine her telling me that no matter what, no matter how bad things seem, she loves me. That's the thing about moms. They're supposed to love

you through everything. There's really nothing like their uncon-
ditional love. Every time I see a mother and daughter together,
doing fun things, love shining from one to another, jealousy rips
through me and it feels like I've swallowed a razor blade.

I'll never have that again.

There's so much I'll never have. It's just not fair.

MARIO

fter waiting for hours, I'm so relieved when I'm
finally fingerprinted and photographed and taken away
from that room. I'm exhausted and I feel like a zombie as we walk
to a different part of the jail. It's cold and the cinder-block walls
are gray and dreary. It smells like ass covered up with Clorox. In
the distance, someone's coughing. Someone else is puking. Someone swears at the guy puking. I decide I'm just gonna be honest.
Maybe he'll reassure me. Maybe he has a son like me at home and
he'll go easy on me.

"I'm scared," I tell the detention officer who's walking with
me. He's a middle-aged white dude and his name tag says Yates.
It's really hitting me that I have to stay here. My throat tingles
and I fight to keep the tears back. He takes me to a little nook
that is curtained off.

"Mind your own business and you'll be fine," Yates tells me.
"Stand here, back against the wall. Now, open your mouth." He
shines a light in my mouth. "Good. Now lift your tongue. All
right." He turns around and goes over to some shelves with
clothes on them. "Now, I need you to take off your pants."

"What? Why?"

"Gotta get you into a jumpsuit."

With my hands still shackled, I unbutton and unzip my tux pants and let them drop to the floor.

"I rented this suit. It needs to go back. Can you get it to my mom?"

He laughs. "First time I've heard that one. Now take off your underwear too."

"Why?"

"Gonna give you some new ones," he says matter-of-factly as he gathers my pants and sets them aside. Then he goes to a pile of light-green briefs, takes a pair, and then goes to a pile of orange jumpsuits and takes one of those too. He sets them on the table near me.

"Now, I'm going to unlock your cuffs briefly." When my hands are free he says, "Finish getting undressed. Take it all off. Even your socks."

When I'm finished and standing there buck naked, shivering, he says, "Now, put on the briefs and the jumpsuit. What size shoe you wear?"

I tell him size eleven and he grabs a pair of the ugliest canvas-and-rubber shoes I've ever seen from a shelf and tosses them on the floor in front of me.

When I'm dressed, he puts the cuffs on me again. "What happens now?" I ask.

"You get a quick medical check. Then I'll take you to the block." He takes a paper bag off the shelf and shoves it into my hands.

The block? What's the block? I want to ask but I feel like that will make me look more stupid and naive than I already do. So I ask, "Will I be alone?" as I peek in the bag. (There's a comb, a toothbrush, a roll of toilet paper, a piece of paper, an envelope, and a soft-tip pen.)

He chuckles. "This ain't the Ritz, kid. Not enough room in our crappy old jail for that. Look, medium-security block is almost like summer camp, okay? You'll be in a room with beds along the walls, a TV everyone loves to fight over, and even a shelf with some books on it. You even get to shit behind a door instead of in your cell. It's not so bad. You'll see."

I want to tell him *Easy for you to say.* But I decide I better quit while I'm ahead.

LUCAS

I wake up at almost noon with a text from Mario's mom.

Something's happened. Can you come down and see me when you get a chance?

I text Mario one of our favorite cat gifs and wait for him to reply with another one we send back and forth to each other, but it never comes. This is not like him. At all.

I've known Mario a long time. His mom too. We live on the same street, and his house is like my second home. It's where we play video games together and watch old episodes of *Battlestar Galactica* with our favorite combination of popcorn and Reese's Pieces mixed together. So after I take the world's fastest shower and throw on some clothes, I run down to Mario's house. Well, that's not exactly true. I'm a big guy, and I don't really run. It's more of a jog/shuffle thing that I do. When I see that Mario's truck isn't in the driveway, I get a funny feeling in the pit of my stomach. Like I ate a bad tuna sandwich or something.

I knock. And when his mom comes to the door, she looks dazed and wounded. Like a bird that's trying to make its way back into the sky after slamming into a windowpane.

The first time I met her, a week or so after we moved into the neighborhood, she offered me a Popsicle. "Can I have an orange one?" I'd asked her.

"You can have whatever color you'd like," she'd replied. And when I wanted another one an hour later, she happily obliged. She's never been like my mom, who is constantly on my case about exercising and eating healthy. When I'm at Mario's, I can just be . . . me. Neither of them ever batted an eye at me for getting up and making myself a sandwich or grabbing a cookie from the cookie jar. At home, I'm like a three-year-old in the kitchen. I have to ask before I can have anything, and unless it's a fruit or vegetable or nuts, the answer is usually no.

"It's so good to see you, Lucas," she says after I give her a hug. A gentle one, because the last thing I want to do is break a wing on the poor bird. "Please, come in and sit down."

She asks if I want anything to eat or drink but all I want to know is what's going on with my best friend.

She takes a deep breath. "Mario is being held at the county jail."

"What? Why?"

"He found Mirabelle's body in the ditch. A deputy was driving by, spotted him, and stopped. Next thing you know—"

I wave my hands in front of me. "Wait, wait, wait. Hold on. Can you back up please? What do you mean he found Mirabelle's body in a ditch?"

"Oh, Lucas, I'm so sorry. I'd forgotten that it's not public knowledge yet. Mirabelle Starr has died. Hopefully they'll release a statement soon. When I spoke to Mario this morning, he told me he wasn't going to say anything to anyone to make sure her parents were notified first. I'm guessing that's happened by now, but still. Until there's a statement from the sheriff's office, we should be careful."

"Mirabelle's . . . dead?" I stare out the window as I try to process this. I can't even . . . How? Why?

"Was it a car accident?" I ask.

"Apparently not," she says. "Mario said he was driving around with Elana when he spotted something in a ditch. He pulled over and not long after, a deputy came along. They're investigating her death now."

I'm in shock. I can't believe someone I go to school with is dead. It doesn't matter that I didn't know her that well, or that I thought she was a little strange sometimes. She was the kind of girl you were just drawn to. Witty, funny and, yeah, pretty. Though she also had a mean streak. I'd witnessed a few things on social media that made me question why so many people seemed to love her. That side of her definitely *wasn't* pretty. Maybe people gave her a pass because her little brother was really sick. Besides, that's high school for you. People say crap all the time they shouldn't be saying.

"So . . . why isn't Mario here? I'm confused. Sorry."

"They've arrested him for supplying alcohol to a minor or something. Apparently, Elana got drunk, though Mario said he didn't give it to her. It doesn't seem to matter to the authorities where she got the alcohol, just that she was intoxicated while in his care."

"They've *arrested* him?" I'm starting to sweat. Perspiration breaks out on my forehead, under my lip, on my neck. It's a Sunday afternoon in May. It's not hot out, not at all, but right now, I feel like I'm in the middle of an inferno.

She stares at the coffee table in front of her. "It's all very confusing to me. That's why I need to find a lawyer."

"They don't think he did it, do they?" I ask. "Killed her? Is that really why they're holding him?"

I think of the stuff that happened last night. The prank played on Mario. The conversations on social media. They don't think that's his motive, do they? He might have been embarrassed, but he'd never kill anyone over something like that. I mean, this is Mario we're talking about. He'd never kill anyone, period.

She keeps staring. Finally, she says, "I don't know."

I stand up. I start pacing. This isn't right, and I can't stand it. "What are you going to do? Can you go down there? Talk to someone?"

"I don't think it'd do any good. He's eighteen. An adult. If they have cause to arrest him, and it seems they do, there's not anything I can do."

I shake my head. "I've seen this before. On TV. They charge him with something to buy them some time while they investigate the thing they're really interested in. Motherf—" I stop just in time. "Sorry. I'm really upset."

She nods. "I know. It's awful. We just have to hope that a good lawyer can get him out of this mess."

"I'll ask my parents if they know anyone," I tell her. "Are they questioning Elana too?"

"I'm not sure. I should probably call her father and see what he has to say. I've just been so focused on trying to find someone to help Mario. I need to retain someone soon. Like, today."

I look over at her, and just as I do, she puts her head in her hands. I think she's about to start crying, and I realize I am not helping at all. In fact, I might be making things worse.

I have no idea what to do. What to say. Nothing like this has ever happened to me before. I'm the guy who spends most of his time doing the same thing, day after day after day. Exactly how I like it.

I wake up. Take a shower. Eat breakfast. Go to school. Go to lunch with Mario. Stop at the store for snacks. Come home. Play video games. Eat dinner. Do some homework. Draw. Eat snacks. Read posts on Reddit. Go to bed.

Once, in middle school, Mom signed me up for a running club.

"It'll be good for you!" she told me with a smile that I wanted to rip off her face like a two-day-old bandage. "You can make new friends and get in shape too. Doesn't it sound like fun?"

I hardly left my room for three days. I went to the bathroom. Brought food from the kitchen back to my room. And that was it—my own private protest.

"I don't want to do any clubs!" I screamed at her when she finally asked why I was so upset. "I don't want to make new friends. And I really, really, *really* don't want to run!"

She gave in. I got my happy routine back. And she never did it again.

But now here I am, staring down the most bizarre situation I could have ever imagined. No. That's not right. I never could have imagined this. My best friend arrested? Possibly suspected of murder?

No. No way.

Underneath all my worry, a memory resurfaces. It's strange, I saw Mirabelle just a few weeks ago, out late. I'd snuck out to go to the convenience store for some snacks—the kind of food my mom refuses to keep in the house. Just as I was walking inside, Mirabelle was leaving the store with some food and batteries.

"Hey," I said, like it was the most normal thing in the world to see her out late buying random items from the store.

She glanced at me, her cheeks turning pink, but she didn't say a word. Then she crawled into the back of an old VW van that had been idling in the parking lot. I didn't get a glimpse of the driver.

I wonder if I should tell someone? It's all so weird and frightening and I want to wish it away. But, of course, life doesn't work that way. My dad loves telling me that.

"Someday you're going to find out life is nothing like the imaginary worlds you live in when you play those stupid games. And then what are you going to do, Lucas? What in the hell are you going to do then?"

Here's what I tell myself: This is Mario. My best friend. My only friend, if you want to know the truth.

I don't know if I have it in me to do anything other than pace and worry, but I decide there's only one way to find out.

"They'll find out who did it," I say as I take a seat next to her. "Then they'll let him go. They'll find the murder weapon or some fingerprints or something. You'll see. It's just gonna take some time, that's all."

She wrings her hands in her lap and stares at them. "I keep picturing him in a jail cell surrounded by a bunch of horrible people. Thieves, rapists, drug dealers. And I just can't . . ." When she leans into me, I tell myself she needs someone to comfort her. I don't want it to be me, but I'm the only one here.

The only one.

Me.

Lucas Simpson.

She sobs as her head falls onto my shoulder. And I gently put my arm around her shoulders and say, "It'll be okay. Mario's the nicest guy I know. It won't stick. Whatever they have on him, it won't stick. We have to believe that."

He's the guy who mowed our lawn and watered our plants when my entire family went to Disneyland last summer for a vacation. We didn't ask him to do it, he just offered. When we came back, he'd even planted some flowers in the bed. Red and purple petunias. He said he thought my mom would like them.

He's the guy who loans me money for lunch when I'm running low. Never asks for it back. Never.

He's the guy who took a girl to the prom because *his mother asked him to*!

Eventually, Ms. Woods walks me to the door. I tell her to let me know if there's anything I can do for her. She promises me that she will.

I tell myself to be ready for anything. Maybe doing things out of my comfort zone will get easier with practice. I can only hope.

PARKER

"Parker, you need to come downstairs, please."

I try to open my eyes, but it feels like someone has glued them shut. Oh, my god. What did I do? Did someone take a hammer to my head last night?

Oh. Right. Not a hammer. Tequila.

"Grandma, I don't feel well," I mumble. "I need to sleep."

"Well, you can't. Some detectives are here to talk to you. Sounds like something happened last night and they have some questions. Parker, I have to tell you, I'm extremely worried right now. Please tell me you're not in any trouble."

"Did you say detectives?" I ask as I force myself to sit up. With one eye barely open, I search the nightstand for my water bottle, but it's not there.

"Yes," she says. "Is there something I should know? About last night?"

I swallow hard and rub my eyes. "I'm sorry. I got into your liquor cabinet after I got home."

She lets out a big sigh. "Oh, Parker. Why'd you do that?"

I shake my head and finally open both eyes. Barely. "Long story. Can you just ask them to come back another time? Please?"

"I don't think that's a good idea," she says sternly as she picks my tux off the floor and puts it on the foot of my bed, my keys in the pocket jingling as she does it. "Clean yourself up, drink some water and get yourself downstairs."

After she shuts my door, I manage to get to my feet and throw on some jeans and a hoodie. I look around for my phone but it's nowhere to be found. I decide I need to worry about that later. I go to the bathroom, where I down a bunch of water, comb my hair and brush my teeth. I feel like the tequila is spilling out of every pore of my body. Will they smell it? God, this is horrible. But there's nothing to do but go down there and see what they want.

I make my way downstairs, where two men with badges hung around their necks stand in the foyer.

"This is my grandson, Parker," Grandma says.

The tall skinny one says, "Parker, I'm Detective Green, and this is Detective Bellinger. Sorry to wake you. Have you heard the news yet?"

"What do you mean? What news?" My heart starts racing. I drank so much last night I can barely remember anything. Did I do something? Oh god, did I drunkenly drive somewhere?

The detective bites his lip, hesitating for just a moment before he says the words. "Mirabelle was found dead in a ditch early this morning."

It takes a moment for it to register. "Wait, what? My Mirabelle?"

"Mirabelle Starr," Detective Green says. "We're very sorry for your loss."

74

One of Grandma's hands covers her mouth while the other clutches her heart. I look around for Grandpa, but he must be at the restaurant, working.

I feel like I'm choking. Drowning. Sinking. I grip the banister like it's a life preserver. Grandma comes over and puts her hand on mine. "Parker, honey, I'm so very sorry."

"Is there somewhere we can sit down?" Bellinger asks.

I somehow make my feet move as Grandma leads us into the front room. The room with the gold sofa and the two red wing-back chairs. The room no one ever sits in except at Christmas-time. I swear even now, in May, there's a slight scent of pine needles. It's always been a place of comfort and joy, with a Christmas tree by the front window and stockings hung on the fireplace mantel. With two haggard investigators staring at me because a girl I love is dead, joy is about as foreign as the mountains of Switzerland.

I take a seat on the sofa but Grandma stays standing, clutching the back of one of the chairs. Green sits at the far end of the sofa while Bellinger takes the other chair.

"I can't believe it," Grandma says, her eyes watering. "What a tragedy. Do you have any idea how it happened?"

Green shoots me a look before he says, "We're not releasing any details yet. Not until we have the official medical examiner's report."

I'm trying to keep it together but it's really hard. I blink back tears and feel like I might get sick right here, in front of everyone.

"Parker?" Grandma says. "Honey, are you okay?"

"No," is all I can say.

"Oh dear, you look so pale. I think you need to try to eat a little something. Let me make you some toast. I'll be right back."

After she leaves, all eyes are on me. Obviously, they're here because they suspect me. I was with her last night, I was her date, for Christ's sake. Everyone saw us together. No disputing that fact. I just wish I could think more clearly.

Bellinger takes out his notebook and Green follows suit.

I clear my throat. "Look, is there, um, any way we could do this later? I'm kind of in shock right now, to be honest."

"Sorry, but we need to do this now," Bellinger says. "It's important we hear from you before too much time passes."

I grab one of the accent pillows and hug it tight. "Okay. Fine." And I then proceed to answer each question to the best of my ability. I tell them we ate dinner here, because Grandpa is a fabulous cook and he offered to make Mirabelle's favorite, veggie lasagna. She loved my grandparents, and she said it didn't matter to her where we had dinner. I think she knew it'd make them happy to be able to share a little bit of the night with us. After that we went to the dance and stayed until around eleven, when we left to go to Jason's house, like so many other people did.

"What time did you leave the party?" Green asks.

"Shortly after midnight."

Bellinger raises an eyebrow. "You didn't stay very long. Is there a reason?"

"Belle insisted on going home. So I took her to her house. And that's when she broke up with me. Right there, in my car."

I can tell it surprises them when I tell them about the breakup.

"Did she say why?" Green asks.

"Nope."

"Think you did something to make her mad?" Bellinger asks.

"The whole night, things were off between us. I can't deny that. But we talked on the way home and I thought we were okay. She knew I was worried about her. She'd been acting strange all night. Actually she'd been acting strange for a while. Still, when she ended it, I was shocked."

"What do you mean, strange?" Green asks. "How so?"

"More irritable than usual, I think. Like, she bit my head off over a silly thing I said when we were getting our official prom photo taken. And she made a big deal about something on Twitter for no reason. It was like she really didn't want to be there, and she took it out on me and everybody else."

"But was she happy to be crowned prom queen?" Bellinger asks.

"I guess so. She was smiling and laughing afterward. She wore the crown or tiara or whatever and had me take a picture of her. But then she checked Twitter and she got weird again. I don't know."

"So when she broke up with you, what'd she say?" Green asks.

"She blurted it out. Said, 'I want to break up, Parker. I'm sorry. I know this is going to hurt you. But it's what I have to do.'"

"What'd you say?" Green asks. "Did you argue about it or anything?"

"It's all kind of a blur, to be honest. I think there was a lot of, 'What do you mean? Why?' She apologized again and said some shit, I mean, stuff, about how she'd always care about me, but this was best for her right now. And before I knew it, she'd jumped out of my car and was running up the driveway to her house."

"What'd you do?" Green asks.

"What could I do? I drove home."

"Did you wait for her to go inside?"

I shake my head. "No. I didn't. I just wanted out of there."

"Do you happen to know if her car was parked in the garage or in the driveway?"

"It was parked across the street from her house, like always. Leaked oil sometimes. She'd been having a lot of trouble with it lately, too. Her grandpa gave it to her—an old Ford Mustang he'd kept from the sixties. Sweet car, but man, what a pain that thing had become lately. Why?"

"We found her car early this morning, broken down not too far from where her body was discovered."

"So she was going somewhere? After I dropped her off?"

"Appears so. Any idea where she might have been headed?"

"None."

Now it's both my head and heart that feel like someone's taken a hammer to them. I put my face in my hands as I mutter more swear words. It's taking everything I have to keep it together.

When I look up again, I tell Green, "I texted her after I got home. Three or four times. Told her I was sorry if I'd done something wrong. I told her if she'd just tell me what it was, maybe I could make it up to her. Told her I loved her. Stuff like that."

"Did she reply at all?"

"Not a word." I swallow, thinking about my missing phone. Where could it be? I silently pray that they don't ask to see it.

Instead, they both nod.

"Did anyone here see you when you came home?" Green asks me. "Your parents or . . . ?"

I sigh and lean my head back, blinking back the tears. "It's just me and my grandparents. And no. They were both in bed."

"So what'd you do?"

I take a deep breath. I should just tell them the truth—I got drunk and passed out. It was stupid. A mistake. But harmless. At least, I think that's the truth. But my memory is still fuzzy from the tequila and the kernel of doubt in my mind makes me want to skip the conversation altogether. "I went to bed."

"What time?" Bellinger asks.

I turn and look out the window. It's nice out today. Sunny. Some of the others probably stayed up all night and went out to breakfast this morning. They're probably just going home now. Why couldn't that be us?

Finally, I turn around and answer their question. "I don't know. I wasn't feeling well so I sacked out on the couch. And then sometime during the night I made it upstairs to my bed. I just . . . I honestly don't remember."

Green leans forward and puts his elbows on his knees. "Parker, are you sure you were here the entire time last night?"

My breathing speeds up and I feel my heartbeat quicken. How am I supposed to answer that question? I got wasted and I was here.

Wasn't I?

I grit my teeth and get to my feet, just as Grandma comes back with a plate of toast. "Look, I know what you're thinking. But I'd never hurt her. Never. I loved her, okay? She meant everything to me. I'm as confused as you are right now. I dropped her off at home and I have no idea how she ended up in a ditch somewhere. It doesn't make sense." I run my hand through my hair. "None of it makes sense, okay?"

My stomach is about to rebel against me, so I run to the bathroom. I didn't think I could feel any emptier than I did last night, but apparently that's just one more thing I was wrong about.

Willow, OR (KATU) — The Richland County sheriff's office reports that eighteen-year-old Mirabelle Elizabeth Starr was found dead early Sunday morning on Wessinger Road. Deputy Wesley Reynolds says Starr had last been seen by her boyfriend at her home, where he dropped her off after attending the junior-senior prom together followed by a party at a friend's house.

The county medical examiner is currently conducting an autopsy to determine the cause of death. Police are actively investigating, and anyone with information regarding the case is urged to contact the sheriff's office immediately.

Donny: Hey, you hear about Mirabelle?

Jason: Yeah. That shit is messed up.

Donny: The police talk to you yet?

Jason: No. Think they will?

Donny: Hell yeah. She was at your party. Right before she died. That's not good.

Jason: She and Parker were arguing before they left. He was not happy when he found her and Mario together. I didn't see how long Mario and her were alone together, did you?

Donny: Nope. Was kinda busy.

Jason: Dude. Are you saying you made cookies in my house last night?

Donny: You know I love cookies

Jason: You dog

Donny: That party was lit

Jason: Glad you had fun but man, I am sick over this Mirabelle business. Can't stop thinking about it.

Donny: School tomorrow's gonna be weird af

Jason: No shit. Think somebody we know did it?

Donny: No idea what to think

Jason: Me either

JOSH

found Mirabelle's note not long after she took off with Parker for prom. She left it in my bathroom, in an envelope under my tube of toothpaste. The outside of the envelope said *Mint (ha, couldn't resist) to be read by Josh and Josh alone.*

God, I miss her so much already.

Now, as I sit here in my room, trying to figure out what to do, all I can think is: it should have been me. God wanted someone from my family, for whatever reason, and it was supposed to be me, but then I got well, so they took her.

Not fair, not fair, not fair.

Mom wants me to eat something. To talk to people who keep coming by to bring food and tell us they're sorry. I have no idea how she and Dad are managing to even walk around right now. I feel like I'm dying all over again. Because she's dead.

Dead. Dead. Dead.

I hate that word. For so long, I thought it was just a matter of time for me. I'd try to imagine what it'd be like to not be here anymore. To not have a body. To not see the sky. To not smell cookies baking in the oven. To not hear the crickets at night. I'd get this weird, panicky feeling every time I tried to imagine just being . . . gone. And now that's what Mirabelle is. Gone. No more seeing. No more hearing. No more smelling. Because someone decided she shouldn't be here anymore.

Why. Not. Me. Instead?

Eventually, I have to get up to pee. Plus, I'm so thirsty. As I head to the bathroom, the doorbell rings. I go in, do my thing, then I gulp down some water.

When I come out, Dad is standing there, his eyes slightly bloodshot and his thinning salt-and-pepper hair sticking every which way. Basically, he looks like crap.

"Josh, we need you to come out here, please."

"Why?"

"The detectives are here to ask us some questions. They may have some for you."

"Dad, I don't think—"

"Son, this is not optional. We have to help them figure out who did this. We *have* to, see? They can't do it without our help."

I sigh. "Fine."

The men aren't in uniform, but they have badges around their necks. Probably so they don't have to keep pulling them out of a pocket and showing them to people.

Mom introduces me to them, Detectives Green and Bellinger.

"We're very sorry for your loss," Detective Green says. "And we know this is a difficult time for you, but it's important we speak to you and get as much information as we can to help us figure out who hurt her."

I can only nod.

Not fair, not fair, not fair.

"We'll sit at the table," Mom says, gesturing for us to take a seat. "Can I get you anything?"

"No, ma'am, we're fine," Detective Bellinger says as he sits in Mirabelle's spot. I look at Mom and Dad, and I know we're all thinking the same thing. But it doesn't matter. She's not here. There's no reason he shouldn't sit there.

They start off asking Mom and Dad about Parker and whether they heard her come inside when he dropped her off. I listen for a minute, but my mind wanders. Back to yesterday afternoon. The last time I saw her.

The last time I'll ever see her.

She'd insisted on getting her dress at a secondhand store in town. She wanted something "vintage." Old, but still nice, I guess? Who knows? Anyway, she walked into the family room wearing a red sleeveless dress with a full skirt, and all three of us, who were sitting on the sofa waiting for her to come out, gasped. I'm not just saying that. We really did. My sister basically lived in Levi's and Chuck Taylors, so to see her dressed up like that was kind of unbelievable.

"What?" she asked us. "What's wrong?"

"Nothing," Mom told her. "Not a thing. I think you've left us sort of speechless."

"Isn't it fabulous?" Mirabelle asked, running her hands down the shiny fabric. "This dress is the only reason I'm even going at this point."

"Oh, honey, are you nervous or something?" Dad asked. "You'll have a great time. You'll see."

"I don't know, I just—"

But she didn't get to finish. The doorbell rang right then. Mom hopped up to get it. It was Parker, of course. When he came in, Mirabelle didn't move. Just stayed in the same spot, in the middle of the front room.

"Wow," he said. "You look . . . amazing."

She muttered a quick thanks, but she kept staring down at her dress. Mom had to remind Mirabelle to get his boutonniere out of the fridge. It was all a little strange.

Mom nudges me back to the present moment. "Did you hear his question, Josh?"

"No. Sorry."

Detective Green says, "I'm wondering if she said anything concerning. Or if she was acting strangely at all? Your parents didn't notice anything, but maybe you did?"

"Yeah," I say, quickly. "What I noticed was that she didn't really want to go to the dance. When Parker walked in, my sister did not seem happy to see him. She even told us the only reason she was excited to be going was because she loved her dress. That seems wrong, doesn't it?"

"Had she and Parker had a fight recently?" Bellinger asks. "Anything like that?"

Mom and Dad look at each other briefly, then back to the detective. "Not that we know of," Mom says. "As far as we knew, everything was fine."

"Any behavior changes recently?" Bellinger asks. "Or problems at school?"

Mom clears her throat. Fiddles with the floral place mat that's sitting in front of her. "Sadly, yes. She hadn't been herself for a while. And her grades had slipped lately. But it'd been a rough year for her. For all of us. I don't know if you know this, but Josh had been really sick for a number of months. She took it hard."

"Who's her closest girlfriend?" Green asks.

"Hm. That'd be Eva London," Mom says. "But she hasn't been around much lately. Not sure why, really. Mirabelle spent most of her free time with Parker."

This is where I should speak up. I start and then I stop. It shouldn't be this hard. I mean, she's gone. It's not like she's gonna get mad at me for telling. She can't. Except I remember those words in her note: *Our secret for now. . . . I don't want to be that girl.* And the look on her face that night not too long ago—the way she begged me.

It was a couple Saturdays ago. I heard a noise in her room. I decided to check it out and that's when I saw her, getting ready to climb out the window.

"You can't tell them," she told me as tears welled up in her eyes. "You can't. They wouldn't understand."

"But where are you going?"

"Out. With friends. That's all."

"But why so late?"

"Josh, please, promise me you won't tell, and I'll give you some of my allowance."

"But, Mir—"

"Promise me, Josh!"

So I did.

Now I just need time to think all this through. It's too soon.

Why do they insist on doing this? It doesn't seem right. They should give us time. A little space. We're not up for this right now.

Detective Green uses a soft voice when he says, "We've found her car and taken it in for evidence."

"Where?" Dad asks. "Where'd you find it?"

"Out on Oldham Road. Not too far from where her body was found. Hood was up. Flashers were on. Appears it broke down."

Now Dad bends his head and I watch as big tears drip down his face. I know what he's thinking—that he should have done more to get her car fixed. Or bought her something more reliable. Something. Anything.

Green continues. "We're going to need to go through her room. We'll be taking some of her things. Anything that might help us with the investigation. I'm sure you understand."

It takes Dad a minute to compose himself. When he finally does, he wipes his face with his hand and says, "Do what you need to do. Have you found her phone?"

"No," Green says. "We've looked, too. We can request records from her cell phone company, though. If you could get us that information, that would be helpful."

Dad gets up. "Sure. I'll get that now."

Tell them.

Tell them.

Tell them.

"Um . . ." is all that comes out.

Everyone looks at me.

"Joshy?" Mom asks. "What is it?"

I swallow hard. "Can I be excused? I don't feel well."

Mom looks at the detectives.

"I think we're done here for now," Bellinger says. "If you think of anything, you can always get in touch with us, okay?"

I nod as I get up and go to my room.

I didn't tell them. I couldn't. Mom and Dad, they'd hate me. I know they would. They'd think it's my fault.

My fault she's dead.

Dead.

LUCAS

Mario and I took Art 1 class together last year. Ever since I was little, I've loved drawing. Monsters, mostly. I've drawn some crazy-ass monsters. There's just something I love about getting lost in a drawing. It's like the rest of the world fades away and all that's left is you and your pencil. And where nothing existed before, something emerges from pure imagination. So amazing. Mario needed some convincing, though. He didn't think art would be a fun class. At all.

"It'll be an easy A," I told him.

"Easy? Lucas, art is not easy unless you're good at it," he argued. "And I am definitely not good at it."

"Maybe it'll be easier after Mr. Hansen teaches us stuff. Like, that's what teachers are supposed to do, right? Teach us things we don't know."

Somehow I managed to talk him into it. But it didn't turn out to be an easy A. In the end, even though Mario did all the assignments and worked really hard on every single one of them, Mr. Hansen gave him a B. When Mario got up the nerve to ask him about it, Mr. Hansen said Mario didn't take his feedback seriously enough.

Mario was not happy. He's a straight-A student, after all. And to get a B in art class? It hurt, I know it did.

"I'm sorry," I told him. "I didn't think—"

"Hey, it's not your fault Mr. Hansen sucks ass," he said at lunch one day. "It's like he's trying to prove a point. It's like he's saying, 'Easy A? Ha, I'll show you, you foolish children of Willow High.'"

"It's savage," I said.

"Mostly sad," Mario said. "You know? Because he had the chance to make me love art. And instead, he made me pretty much hate it."

Even though Mario didn't blame me, I felt like the worst friend in the world for about a week. I think he got over it way sooner than I did. It wasn't long before we were joking about it. Because what else can you do, really?

"Hey, Mario, what classes did you decide to take next term?"

"Oh, you know, thought I'd give AP Physics a try. It's gotta be easier than art class, right?"

I'm thinking about all this on my way home from Mario's house. A path I've walked a thousand times and hope to walk a thousand more. There's the Lindens' yard, filled with gnomes. And the Johnsons' yard that's so overgrown, if they finally mowed it down, an army of rats and raccoons would probably protest. This town isn't much, that's for sure, but I've never really minded because I had Mario and his mom.

Man, a B in art class seems so freaking tame now. Like, for most of Mario's high school career, that one stupid grade was about as bad as it got.

Not anymore.

I retreat to my room and pull out a sketch pad. My pencil flies across the page as I draw a man in armor with a sword. A beautiful, shiny steel machete, almost as big as he is. Coming at him is a monster, claws up and baring his teeth. I imagine Mario under that armor. Ready to battle. To fight for his life. But the monster is too big. Too powerful. So I draw another man in armor. This one doesn't have a fancy sword, though. Just a small hunting sword. But he has something else. Something better. He commands an army behind him. Hundreds and hundreds of men in the distance, ready to battle with just one command.

When I'm finished, I study the picture for a long time. It feels like there's something missing. I add more details to the swords. Fill in the shadows a tiny bit more. Add more marks in the background—marks that represent the army. My army.

And then, after I stare at it for I don't know how long, I write three words across the top, in block letters.

Battle for Truth.

JASON

"Good afternoon," the short man with a mustache says. "I'm Detective Bellinger. And this is Detective Green. We're criminal investigators with the county. We'd like to talk to your son, Jason, if he's here?"

I'm standing back, watching my father talk to these guys at the door.

"What is this about?" my father asks.

"One of your son's schoolmates was found dead last night," the tall one, Green, says. "Witnesses say she was here at your house before she died. I need to ask Jason some questions about that."

Dad opens the door. "Please. Come in." He turns around, probably to call my name, but I'm standing right there. "Detectives, this is my son, Jason. Son, why don't you show these two gentlemen to the table?"

Mom is in the kitchen doing dishes. I know she heard everything. Sound carries easily in this house.

"Can I get either of you some coffee?" she asks. "Just made a fresh pot."

"That would be great," Green says. "Been up all night."

"I'll take one too, please," Bellinger says.

"Cream or sugar?"

"Black is fine, thank you," Green says. Bellinger nods in agreement.

I take a seat at the table. Dad sits down too. Doesn't ask if it's okay, just does it. My parents know I had a party. They stayed at my grandparents' house across town for the night so they wouldn't worry about us and I wouldn't worry about them. We didn't discuss the prospect of someone bringing alcohol, but it *was* prom night. They can't be that naive, can they?

We have a huge house and they figured people would want to go somewhere after prom. So they offered it up. I didn't invite the whole class. Hell, no. I think I had fifty people here? Maybe? I know some couples got hotel rooms, while others went out for dessert at Shari's.

Mostly, it was a good time. Well, until somebody got the bright idea to start blasting music from their car parked outside. A couple of girls were dancing on the hood, like some bad eighties music video. Yeah, it got a little wild, unfortunately. And it all went downhill from there.

"Jason, have you heard about Mirabelle Starr?" Green asks. Shit, he looks young. How does someone that young get to be detective, anyway?

I nod. "Unfortunately, yeah. It's been all over social media."

"Right," Bellinger says. "She was seen here last night. Did you talk to her at all?"

"We said a few words," I tell him as Mom brings over the two cups of coffee and sets them on the table. Then she takes a seat. Both of the detectives reach for a cup and immediately start drinking.

After Bellinger sets his cup down, he pulls a notebook from his coat. "How'd she seem to you?"

"What do you mean?"

"Did she seem happy? Sad? Upset?"

I shrug. "I said hello to her and her boyfriend, Parker. They got here just as the party was starting to pop. People everywhere, some of them dancing. I told them there was some food and drink in the kitchen and to help themselves. She didn't say anything. Parker thanked me. She seemed a little distant. Maybe. I don't know. Not her usual talkative self, I guess. Parker turned toward the kitchen. She followed him. I didn't go in there with them. I'm not sure what happened after that."

"Did you see her talking to Mario Woods at all?" Green asks.

"It's funny you ask that. I saw them coming out of my bedroom. I don't know how long they were in there or anything, though. I'm guessing not long, since both of their dates were at the party too. And when Parker saw them together, he was not happy."

"What do you mean?" Bellinger asks.

I look at Dad. He tells me, "You need to be honest. I know Parker is your friend, but this is important, son. Just tell them what you saw and heard."

I nod. "Parker yelled at her. Said he'd been looking all over for her. Mirabelle tried to explain that she'd just wanted to apologize to Mario about what she'd said on social media. 'We needed to clear the air.' That's what she said. Then Parker said he was pretty sure they didn't need to do that behind a closed door."

96

"So he sounded suspicious?" Bellinger asks. "Like he didn't believe she just wanted to apologize?"

I stare at my hands. "That's right."

"Did Mario come to her defense or anything?"

I look up again. "No. He kind of snuck off, actually. Like he didn't want anything to do with it. And since people were starting to gather around, Parker asked me if they could borrow my room for a while to talk. I told him he could have it for as long as he needed."

"Hmm. Okay," Green says. "So they go in there to talk. Did you see them after that?"

"Yeah. A while later, Mirabelle stormed out of the house and Parker followed her. I think it was just a big misunderstanding. Look, he's a friend and I know he really loved her. He's gotta be upset about what happened. Especially if they ended the night arguing with each other."

"Were either Parker or Mirabelle drinking?" Bellinger asks. This guy has piercing brown eyes. Whenever I look at him, it feels like he's looking deep inside my soul. Creepy.

"I don't know."

Dad looks at me. "Drinking? Jason, something you want to tell us?"

"Some people were sneaking it in, I guess. Sorry."

Thank god Detective Bellinger interjects before Dad can drill me anymore about it. "What about Mario and Elana? Did you see them leave?"

"Actually, yeah, I did. It was shortly after Mario and Mirabelle came out of my room. I remember because the king and the queen get these corny crowns, and Elana wore Mario's. As Mario and Elana were trying to leave, someone took it off her head and people were playing keep-away with it."

"You remember what time that was?" Green asks.

"It was pretty early. Like, at least an hour before the deputy came and broke up the party."

"An hour?" Bellinger asks. He writes down something in his notebook. "You sure about that?"

"Yep."

"They say anything about where they were going?" Green asks.

"No. Nothing like that. When Mario finally got the crown back, I walked them to the door. Mario said he'd see me Monday in physics. I joked with him. Asked if I could borrow his notes for the test on Friday. He's one of the smartest kids in that class."

"Did you notice anything strange about either Elana or Mario?"

"Strange?"

"Sorry. I mean, out of the ordinary?"

I shrug. "No. Not that I can think of."

"You know him very well? Mario?" Green asks.

"He doesn't play sports, so no. He's smart. Quiet. To be honest, you hardly notice him most of the time. I think that's why so many people voted for him to be prom king. He's a really nice guy. One of those people you hope good things for, you know?"

"Did you notice either of them drinking?" Bellinger asks.

"They weren't," I say. "Not at first, anyway. People were giving Elana a bad time about it."

"What do you mean? How come?"

"They love picking on that girl for some reason. They were

calling her Miss Goody-Goody. Later, someone gave her some minibar liquor bottles. Right before she left, she opened one, took a big swig, and then stuck it in her purse along with the unopened ones. 'Happy now?' she yelled. A few clapped or cheered while a bunch of people just laughed. When they left, I was kind of relieved, to be honest."

"Do you know who gave her the alcohol?" Bellinger asks.

"No, sorry."

The two detectives look at each other and I can't help but wonder why that particular comment is so interesting to them.

"What was the deal with Mirabelle's comments on social media last night?" Green asks. "Know anything about that?"

"Not really." I know if I don't explain what he's talking about, Mom and Dad will ask about it. "On Twitter, Mirabelle told Elana she should keep her mouth closed if Mario kissed her good night. And I think that made everyone assume Mirabelle and Mario had kissed at some point. Which was surprising to me. And from Parker's tweet, it sounds like he didn't know about it either."

"Did you believe her when she said she'd wanted to apologize to Mario for that?" Bellinger asks.

I shrug. "Yeah, I guess so. I mean, what else could they have been talking about?"

"You don't think something . . . funny was going on between the two of them?" Green asks.

I can't help it. I laugh. "No! There's no way. Like I said, their dates were there. I'm guessing it was like a five-minute conversation, at most. And besides, you gotta understand, Mario is not a player. He's quiet. Studious, you know? He was nominated Prince of Intellect. That's why we were all so surprised about Elana. We couldn't believe he asked her. It was the talk of the school for, like, a week."

"Was there something specific that made the matchup so surprising?" Bellinger asks.

I look at my mom as I try to figure out the right words. Her eyes are warm. Encouraging. I turn back and look at the piercing brown eyes of the detective. "It's kind of hard to explain. Just didn't seem like his type, I guess. A lot of people can't stand her, for some reason. But it's not just that people don't like her—she's standoffish, likes to keep to herself. And then you have Mario, the nice guy everyone likes. I mean, he's quiet too, but still, they just seem really different. I think that's why people were so shocked that he asked her."

"Okay," Green says. "Is there anything else you can think of that might be helpful? Anything that seemed out of the ordinary to you? Anything you heard that didn't seem right? From anyone who was here last night?"

I shake my head. "Nah. It's unbelievable, really. Mirabelle, dead? If you ask me, there's no way it was someone from the party. I don't think anyone I know would want to see her hurt. At all."

Green shuts his notebook. Pulls a folded-up piece of paper out of his pocket. Slides it over to me, along with his pen.

"I'm going to need a list of the names of everyone who was here last night."

"Everyone?" I ask. "I don't know—"

"Do your best. It's important, Jason. We need to get to the

bottom of this, and the more kids we talk to, the better our chances of doing that."

"Okay. Yeah. Just their names or . . . ?"

"Full names and phone numbers for any of them you know."

Then Green slides a card over to me. "And if you think of anything that might be helpful after we leave, this is my number. Please call me. Day or night. All right?"

"Yeah. Sure."

But what does he think I might remember? Someone walking out of here with a steak knife? That thought makes me ask the question, "Do you know . . . I mean, is it clear how she died?"

"An autopsy is being performed," Bellinger says as he tucks his notebook away. "We hope to have the results by tomorrow. We're not giving out any details until then."

No matter how it was done, it's hard to imagine anyone hurting her. Not Mario. Not anyone I know. There's just no way.

DETECTIVE GREEN

A homicide here, in little Willow, Oregon. On prom night, of all nights, with a hundred moving pieces we have to try to put together. When we were asked who wanted to take the lead, Bellinger said, "Not me."

He's got some personal stuff going on at home. His mother is in hospice care and his oldest son lost his job recently and moved with his family back home to live in the basement. Since the closest thing I have to a family is the old lady, Flora, who lives next door and occasionally asks me to read to her and walk her hundred-year-old Pomeranian, I volunteered.

"It's not like I'm gonna leave you high and dry," Bellinger told me. *Sure as hell hope not*, I thought.

When we leave the kid Jason's house, there are a couple of things I can't shake.

"That was fairly enlightening," I say to Bellinger as we get into the black sedan we're driving.

"Sure was. He says Elana hadn't been drinking most of the night and that they left the party much earlier than we'd been told."

"And then we've got the two of them, Mario and Mirabelle,

alone for a short period of time. What if she said something that made things worse between the two of them instead of better?"

"That's definitely a possibility. But we've also got the jealous boyfriend who didn't say a word about him finding Mario and Mirabelle together at the party."

Bellinger starts the car and backs out of the driveway while I buckle up. "Copy that. So, he's already pissed about finding the two of them together. And then she breaks up with him. But why go after her and not Mario, then?"

"Like we're supposed to know what a killer is thinking in that moment of rage? Could be he set out to find either one of them. Maybe he came upon Mirabelle, her car broken down along the side of the road, and that's all it took if he needed that anger to go somewhere."

It's quiet for a while. Eventually, Bellinger says, "I can't stop thinking about Mario, though. The guy who was found at the crime scene. You think he made another stop? After they left the party?"

"He certainly had time," I say.

"We need to get back to his truck," Bellinger says. "Process it for trace evidence."

"Yeah. Glad we decided to have it towed away on the flatbed. I want to really scour that thing. I don't know why, but something tells me we're going to find something." I think about the other part of the equation. The part we haven't discussed much. "But what about Elana? If Mario did it, you think she had anything to do with it?"

"She may not have been intoxicated when she left the party, but she did drink more than just a sip of that alcohol she had in her purse. Breathalyzer said so. My question is, why drink after the party?"

"Maybe Mario encouraged it. Wanted to get her so drunk she'd pass out and give him an opportunity to commit the crime without any eyes on him."

"You talked to Mario," he says. "Does he seem like the type who would do something like this?"

I scratch my chin. "You know who he reminds me of? That kid a few years back. The dropout who was dealing drugs at the middle school. Seemed nice. Soft-spoken. Had a logical answer for everything. After I talked to him, I couldn't believe he'd be doing something like that. Nothing he said sounded suspicious. His high school teachers spoke highly of him too. Sure, they were disappointed when he dropped out, but said he had a bad family situation going on and they understood. It happens a lot, they said. And so, after I questioned him because of a tip, I let him go. Can't tell you how badly I wanted a do-over later."

"We don't get do-overs in this business, though," Bellinger says.

"Don't I know it. And I've always wondered how many more kids got hurt after that. Got hooked on drugs. After my mistake."

It's quiet for a minute before he says, "If we look at motive alone, Parker makes a lot more sense. He'd just been dumped."

"I'll pull up Mario's Twitter account and see what was going on with that. If he was pissed at Mirabelle for talking smack about him, that also gives him a motive."

"I swear, social media will be the death of our society," Bellinger says. "It's all fun and games until it's not."

"True that."

ELANA

When Daddy sees me, I can tell he's trying to keep his emotions in check. His bottom lip trembles as he attempts a smile. He pulls me to him and holds me like I'm the only thing that can keep him from drowning. And maybe I am.

After he finally lets go, he says, "Elana, are you all right?"

"I'm fine. Just really, really tired. Can we go home now, please?"

"Absolutely. You got everything?"

I wave my handbag at him. "Yep. All here."

I can't believe how bright it is outside. I hold my hand over my eyes to try to block some of the rays. It's odd how last night now feels like a lifetime ago.

We get into Daddy's BMW, and before he starts the car, he pulls out a hanky and wipes his face. Then he turns and looks at me. "Honey, you sure you're okay?"

"Yes. I'm sure."

"Did they treat you all right? If you say no, I swear—"

"Please don't worry. They kept me in a room by myself. Brought me some tea and water. They were pretty nice, actually. Asked me a ton of questions. I was so relieved when they finally said they were releasing me."

"They told me they gave you a citation. Minor in possession. Elana . . ."

His voice trails off.

"Are you mad?" I ask.

He sighs. "I don't know, kiddo. The range of emotions I've felt since you first called have run the gamut. Anger was probably in there at one point, yes. But I think right now, in this moment, I'm just relieved you're safe and out of there and coming home."

"Have you heard anything about Mario?" I ask. "Is he going home too?"

He starts the car and then looks at me. His face suddenly changes. Concern replaces relief once again. "His mom called me. He's been arrested. I think he'll have to stay until he can get in front of a judge tomorrow."

"Arrested? For what? Murder?"

He gives me a strange look. "Murder? No. Of course not. Janice said it's for contributing to the delinquency of a minor and possession of an open container."

"Oh, my god," I say as I look at the scenery going by. "They're arresting him because of me."

He pulls out of the parking space. "I should say that Janice is concerned there might be more going on than we know, however. Like maybe there is some suspicion around him and Mirabelle, so they're holding him while they look for evidence. That is really messed up if that's the case." He pauses. "You told them nothing happened, right?"

I press my fingertips into my closed eyelids. Shit. This is all too much. "I told them I didn't see or hear anything strange. Mostly because I kind of . . . passed out."

"On the way home, you mean?"

"Yeah."

"What's happening to Mario is really serious, Elana," Dad says. "If there's anything they should know, something you aren't telling them, you need to fix that."

"There's nothing I can tell them that would help him. I swear. We left the party. We drove around for a while. I was out of it. He found the body. The cops came and took us in. That's it."

"I wish he'd just brought you home," Dad says. "Why didn't he do that?"

I know I should answer him, but instead I tune him out. I need a break from thinking about everything.

On my phone, I scroll through Instagram. It's full of photos from prom. So many happy people. I think of Mario, stuck in that miserable jail, knowing the last thing he's feeling right now is happiness.

I did my best to help. The rest is up to him.

Elana @elanadex
Mario got arrested. For contributing to the
delinquency of a minor. As in, contributing to the
delinquency of me. I feel terrible.

Lucas @lucaspucas
@elanadex I'm livid on my friend's behalf. He
doesn't belong in jail.

Donny @DonnyB43
@lucaspucas @elanadex JFC, he's in jail? That is
savage.

Elana @elanadex
They took me in for questioning about what
happened last night but let me go. I wish I could
do something.

Jason @jajumps23
Detectives were here questioning me. I had to give
them a list of who was at the party. They may come
and talk to any of you. Be ready. Let's help find the
asshole who killed her. #justiceformirabelle

Donny @DonnyB43
#justiceformirabelle

Parker @parker_brands

#justiceformirabelle

Lucas @lucaspucas

#justiceformirabelle but let's not forget
#justiceformario too

MARIO

Free.

A word I hadn't thought about much until now.

Before all this, I was free to work my butt off at the Pay-n-Pak for minimum wage. Free to read all the graphic novels I could handle. Free to scream in terror when a spider of any size entered my personal space. Free to ask a girl to go to prom with me. Free to go to my dream college, University of Washington, and study software engineering so I can develop apps that might make a difference in people's lives.

Maybe I should have told the deputy about my plans. Told him how hard I worked on my college essays so U of W wouldn't be able to say no. Made him see that I'm not the conniving criminal he thinks I am.

I crawl onto a cold, hard metal bunk and try to sleep, but it's so noisy it doesn't take long for me to realize there's no way that's happening. Still, I'm not moving. I may just stay right here until Monday when I can get out, see the judge, and go home.

It's Sunday. I should be home, helping Mom with groceries and cooking meals for the week. Days off from work vary during the week, but they always give me Sundays off. It's the day I catch up on homework and spend time with Mom. I didn't like cooking with her at first. It seemed tedious. Boring. But somewhere along the way, I started to like it.

"What should we add to the chili to try to spice it up?" she asked last week.

"How about cinnamon?" I joked.

"Mario, that's not a bad idea, actually. Let's try a little. See what happens."

I didn't think it tasted any different, but she swore it was a brilliant addition to the recipe.

While we cook, we usually play music from the seventies, which she has always loved and which grew on me after watching one of my favorite movies, *Guardians of the Galaxy*. We sing a mean duet of "Come and Get Your Love."

Of course, with the meal prep comes a whole bunch of dishwashing, and there isn't a single thing I like about that. I whine about it every time and my mother never lets me out of it. Never.

"You can't have the good food without the dirty dishes," she said once. After thinking about it for a minute, she followed up with, "Wow. I feel like that's a perfect metaphor for life."

I guess I'm doing the dishes now for my eighteen years of delicious food. My stomach growls and I realize I need to think about something else. I'm so hungry, I'd take some chili flavored with that ridiculous pumpkin spice if someone offered it to me right now.

Someone says, "Hey, prom king. You okay?"

When I hear it, I wonder who in here could possibly know that about me? When I look up, I discover Jenius standing there, smirking at me. Except he's now wearing the same stylish jump-suit that I am.

"I actually was prom king, if you can believe it." I sit up. "And sure, I'm freakin' fantastic. Didn't you hear? This place is like sum-mer camp?"

It makes him smile. "Yeah, I've been here a couple of times. It's definitely like summer camp. Lots of fresh air. Wonderful, healthy food. Cute chicks." He chuckles. "Hey, at least you don't have your mom screaming at you to clean your room all day long, right?"

"My mom doesn't scream," I say. "And even if she did, pretty sure that'd be ten times better than this place."

My stomach rumbles again. They gave us Hot Pockets to eat while we waited for hours in the booking cell, but that's the only thing I've eaten in a long time. Hard to believe last night I was eating a juicy steak alongside garlic mashed potatoes and today I'm eating jail food. Man, what I'd give for an ice-cold Pepsi and a juicy cheeseburger.

"What's your name, kid?"

"Mario."

"I'm Willy. What are you in for?"

"Contributing to the delinquency of a minor," I say. "Although I also found a dead girl in a ditch, so that could be part of it too. I'm pretty confused about what's going on, to be honest."

He stares at me. The corners of his mouth curl up. "Of all the things you could have said, I was not expecting that. Someone working on getting you a lawyer?"

"Yeah. My mom said she is."

"Get a good one," he says sternly.

"Yeah. Okay." I pause. "There are a lot of things I'd change about last night if I could, and I won't lie, it's eating me up inside. But I didn't kill anyone. I swear."

He chuckles. "You know that's what they all say, right?"

"They do?"

"Oh yeah. No one ever admits anything. Unless they're stupid, I guess. Don't be stupid. Stick to your story. That's the best advice I can give you right now. Stick to it and don't let anyone fluster you. You change even one tiny detail at this point, it'll look really bad."

"But I—"

He doesn't let me finish. "Didn't do it. Yeah. I know. You said that already."

I take a deep breath and say, "What about you? What brings you to this delightful place?"

"Just the usual," Willy says. "Drugs."

I don't know what to say, so I simply nod. "Well, I'm gonna try to sleep until dinner," I tell him. "I'm beat."

"Yeah. Okay."

He walks away and I think about what that must be like—to be arrested so much you actually say, "Just the usual." I swear, when I get out of here, I am going to live the cleanest life anyone has ever seen. I don't even want to play *Call of Duty* anymore. Lucas is going to have to be satisfied playing *Kirby* and *Mario Kart* from now on.

Mario "Good Boy" Woods, that'll be me.

DETECTIVE GREEN

As I record the notes on my computer from the interviews we've done so far, my mind is scrambling to put the pieces together. Solving a crime like this is all about connecting the dots until the killer has a big fat bull's-eye centered on him.

Like Bellinger said, Mirabelle's boyfriend, Parker, would be the logical suspect. After all, they left the party fighting. And the girl broke up with him right after. We probably need to go back and talk to him some more. Press on him harder.

Parker says they left the party around twelve-thirty. I'm guessing he's off on that by about ten minutes if he was home no later than one. Rarely do people remember the time exactly. So he took Mirabelle home, she broke up with him, which he said didn't take long, and then he drove to his house. No one in Mirabelle's family heard her come in, and from the looks of things, that's probably because she didn't enter the house at all. She waited for Parker to leave and then she likely got in her car and drove off.

If someone came upon her on that back-country road with her car broken down, that person is probably the killer. Somehow, we need evidence that tells us who that was.

"Hey," Bellinger says as he walks up to my workstation. "We got something."

I look at him. "Something good?"

He nods. "I'd say so. Found a couple of blond hairs in the back of that kid's truck, along with Mirabelle's prints."

"Damn. And here I was just thinking we should go back to the boyfriend's house."

"Mirabelle was in Mario's truck," he says. "You were right, man. Your gut was right."

I don't want to get this one wrong. I *can't* get this one wrong. I'd never forgive myself.

"So he lied to me." I don't try to hide my anger. "He didn't say a word about talking to her at the party or about her being in his truck. That's definitely a sign he's hiding something."

"What's odd is that she wasn't in the front. Only Elana's prints were found there."

"Why the back?" I say, thinking out loud. "Why wouldn't she just squeeze into the front? She's skinny as a twig. She could have easily fit."

Bellinger reaches down and takes a mint from the candy dish I keep there. He's got a problem with bad breath, something I've been nagging him about for years. Good to see he's not completely oblivious.

I continue. "Maybe . . . maybe he picks her up because her car's broken down and she climbs in the back because Elana is passed out in the front. When they reach her destination, he pulls over to let her out and she gets another dig in about what happened between them. And this time, he snaps."

"Why'd Mirabelle leave her house in the first place?" Bellinger asks. "Where was she going? That's the big question."

"One thing at a time. What about the hair? Can we send it in for DNA testing?"

"Already done," he replies. "But you can guess how that will probably go."

I can. DNA from a piece of hair is impossible unless the hair has the follicle on it. In other words, it can only be tested if it was pulled out from the root, and that usually isn't the case. It also takes a good two weeks to get results back.

"The thing is," I tell Bellinger, "if it's not hers, whose would it be? He doesn't have a girlfriend, which is why he took Elana to the prom, right?"

There's no answer. Instead, he says, "Wish we had Mirabelle's cell phone. Would really help us to paint a picture of what went on last night."

"We searched the scene extensively," I say with a yawn. Damn, it's been a long day. So many interviews I feel like I could go a week without talking and be happy as a clam. Or a monk. Or a mime. "If it's not in her car or on her, guessing we'll never find it. Someone probably made damn sure of that. What about her laptop?"

"I have Ryder going through it along with Mario's. We'll see if anything turns up. What about their cell phone carriers?"

"Yeah. They want court orders to release the records. I'll get that first thing tomorrow."

Bellinger chews on his bottom lip. "I think it's time to talk to him. Mario, I mean. Put some pressure on him. Maybe I can get him to confess. Put an end to all this bullshit."

"I bet he's lawyering up as we speak," I say. "I'd be. Wouldn't you?"

He chews on the mint. "What do you think? What's your gut telling you?"

"Mario was found at the crime scene. Standing there, as in, not doing a damn thing. He didn't try to help her. He didn't call for medical. Earlier that night, he was humiliated, big time. In front of everyone. Someone even got it on video and the thing went viral. From the stuff I read, it sounds like Mirabelle was likely behind the whole thing. And even if she wasn't, it reads like Mario thought she was. Not to mention the two had some kind of history. And now we have evidence she was in his truck. What else do we need?"

"I haven't looked at the social media stuff," Bellinger says. "I'll do that now. Then I'm heading out. You should do the same. It's been one helluva day. There's always tomorrow, right?"

In law enforcement, that is definitely true. It never ends.

DOREEN STARR

"Mom?"

I bolt upright, my heart racing. I scan the room, hoping it's real. Hoping *she's* real.

But it's not her. How could it be? I suppose my brain heard what it wanted to hear.

"Sorry," Josh says. "I shouldn't have woken you."

"No, honey, it's okay," I say as I brush my messy hair out of my eyes and try to breathe away the pain of waking up to this nightmare again. "Do you need something? Are you hungry?"

"No, it's just . . ."

I look up at him. His face is splotchy. Has he been crying? I pat the bed, *her* bed, signaling to take a seat. "I didn't mean to fall asleep," I tell him as he steps forward. "I came in here to . . ."

My voice trails off. Anything I say next will sound weird. Smell her? Be near her? Feel closer to her? I blink back the tears. *Not now. Be strong. Be strong for him. He needs you right now.*

Josh sits down. "It's okay," he says as if he senses why I'm hesitating. "You don't have to explain. Mom, did you know Mirabelle was gonna break up with Parker last night?"

I shake my head. "What? No. She wouldn't do that to him."

"Parker's grandma brought us a casserole while you were sleeping, and she told Dad that's what happened. He took her home and she broke up with him."

I can hardly wrap my head around this. Why would Mirabelle do that? They were so happy together. Weren't they? "Did Parker's grandma say how he was doing?"

"Not very well. Won't come out of his room since the detectives questioned him. I can't stop thinking about them since they left here. The detectives, I mean. You think they'll be able to figure out who did it?"

I can hardly keep it together as I look at my boy who has gone through so much. The fact that he has to go through this on top of everything else hurts me more than anything else right now. I put my hand on his cheek. "They're doing their very best, I know that."

"There's something else."

I brace myself. "What? What is it?"

"On social media, they're saying the guy who was crowned prom king has been arrested."

It feels like the floor has dropped out from beneath me. "Arrested? You mean . . . they think he did it?"

Josh shrugs. "It doesn't sound like that's what it is, but I'm not really sure. Isn't that kind of weird, though? That the prom king is in jail after the prom queen is found dead?"

"Yes," is all I can manage to say.

He's quiet for a moment. "I still can't believe it. It doesn't seem . . . real."

"I know it doesn't." My phone buzzes on the nightstand next

to me. I pick it up, and when I see I have lots of messages, I set the phone back down. I think I've officially reached my limit for the day. Thank god Jerry is out there handling the people who stop by without asking first.

Josh points to my phone. "What are people saying?"

"Sending their love and prayers. Wanting to know how we're doing. A few want to hear more about what happened."

"Like it's any of their business."

I scoot around him and stand up. "Come on. It's almost dinnertime. We should probably try to eat something."

"Mom?"

I look at him. "Hmm?"

"This seems so unfair. After everything with me. Now this."

"We just have to take it one day at a time. And lean on each other. Okay?"

"I was wondering . . . I kind of . . . feel like playing the drums," he says. "But I don't want to bother you guys."

"Are you kidding?" I put on my best smile for this kid I love with my whole heart. "We love hearing you play."

There will be enough silence in the coming days. I wish I played. Pounding on something sounds pretty good about now.

PARKER

was upset, not angry.

Distraught. Heartbroken. Sad.

Not angry about her breaking up with me.

Sure, I was angry about her and Mario sneaking off to talk, but she explained it and I told myself I needed to do my best to trust her. Believe her.

She'd said she needed to clear the air between them. Said she was trying to get her life right and she realized at the party she needed to start being her true self.

But then she broke up with me, and everything I thought and believed flew out the window. Even now, I can't shake the fact that these past couple of months, something was different with Belle. Whenever I asked her why she seemed distant, she'd blame it on her brother.

"You don't know what it's like," she'd told me once. "To have someone you love with your whole heart so sick that he could have died. It changes you. And if you don't like it, no one is making you stay."

We had lots of little arguments like that. She'd get upset, I'd feel horrible and apologize for even asking, and then I'd spend the next few days trying to make it up to her.

Maybe I was wrong to try to believe her. What if Mario asked her to ditch me and meet up with him somewhere? Why else would she leave after I dropped her off? Just thinking about it—her and him together—makes me want to punch something. Hard.

Last night, in a drunken stupor, did I imagine them together? Could that have triggered something in me? I've always thought people who don't have a good support system are the ones who get in trouble. Like, they don't have anyone to talk to, so they let the anger build up over time until it boils over, and they do something "in a fit of rage."

I wish I could remember. I've tried so hard, but I don't recall getting up off the couch, walking upstairs, taking off my clothes, or getting into bed. So if I don't remember any of that, I know there's more I could be forgetting.

Plus, I can't find my phone anywhere. Could it be out *there*?

I've got to be at the top of their list at this point, based on motive alone. Maybe I shouldn't have told them about the breakup. If only Grandma or Grandpa could vouch for me. But it's not on them, I know that. I'm the one who came home and made the choices I did. I wish I could go back and change so many things, but this isn't *Back to the Future*. What's done is done, and all I can do is stay calm and try not to look guilty.

Mario's arrest is all over social media. Maybe he's at the top of their list too. If they want to pin it on him and that helps keep their eyes off me, I have no problem with that.

I keep wishing I could hear Belle's voice. The way I feel, knowing she's gone forever, I just don't see how I could have hurt her. Killed her. I loved her too damn much.

DETECTIVE GREEN

Two calls come in right before I'm about to go home.

The first is the one we've been waiting for. The medical examiner calls and gives me the important points of the autopsy, performed by a state forensic pathologist. There will be more information in the coming days, once the lab results come back and whatnot. But for now, he gives me what we need the most.

He says, "Body temperature, rigor and livor mortis and stomach contents approximate the time of death between twelve-thirty and two-thirty a.m. on May fifteenth. Immediate cause of death is asphyxia due to ligature strangulation. Victim has scratch marks on the neck and under the chin, consistent with trying to remove the item used for cutting off the oxygen supply. Full report to come, of course."

I thank him and hang up.

Ligature strangulation means something besides someone's hands was used to cut off the oxygen supply. I'm pondering what that might mean, if anything, when another call comes through, transferred from the main line.

"Detective Green," I say.

"I know who killed the girl," a deep, husky voice says.

It sounds fake. Like someone is putting it on. Trying to mask their own voice. Caller ID on my desk phone reads *Private.* They probably dialed sixty-seven in order to make the call anonymously.

"Killed who?" I ask.

"Mirabelle."

"How do you know?"

"Mario Woods did it. He murdered her."

"Your name, please?"

The caller hangs up.

We have evidence from his truck that confirms Mirabelle was in the back. We have a motive from events that happened earlier in the evening. Now we have an anonymous caller saying he did it.

That poor girl was brutally murdered at someone's hands. She was on a country road alone and trusted someone with her life. Who else could it be, if it wasn't Mario? According to him, he was driving around at the exact time her car broke down. The timeline adds up. And if he didn't hurt her, if he just gave her a ride somewhere, why lie about it?

Still, doubt niggles at me. The thing is, though, with this job, it's always there. Always. When I let myself lean into it, it becomes bigger than it should be. I start making excuses, like I did for that other kid. And as soon as that happens, I'm screwed.

I have to look at what I have, and right now, all signs point in one direction. I'm guessing he acted out in a moment of fury and probably regretted it as soon as it was over.

Christ. What a story this will make. Headlines will go crazy for it: prom king suspected of killing prom queen after social media drama. Nothing I can do about any of that, though. It is what it is.

I sit back down at my desk and send an email to the district attorney, telling him I'll be at his office first thing tomorrow morning.

We need to arrest Mario Woods for the murder of Mirabelle Starr.

MARIO

"Woods."

I wake up with a start, but then I lie back, wondering if I dreamed it. I hadn't been asleep long. I'd gone back to my bunk after a breakfast of Cream of Wheat, canned fruit, a slice of whole-wheat bread and some milk and juice.

"Woods!"

I jump to my feet. My heart is pounding, but I tell myself this is the first step of getting out of here and going home. Either I'm going to see my lawyer or I'm going to see the judge. Whichever it is, I'll be home soon. That's what I have to focus on.

A detention officer walks me out of the block. He has handcuffs waiting for me, which I assume is procedure. But then he says, "Mario Woods, you are under arrest for the murder of Mirabelle Starr."

He reads me my rights but all I can hear is the word *murder* repeating in my head, over and over again.

"But I didn't do it!" I yell. "Hold on. What's happening? Where are we going?"

"We need to get you booked. New crime, new booking. Then

you'll be moved to maximum-security block. Summer camp's over for you, kid."

Holy shit. Maximum-security block?

"My mom was supposed to get me a lawyer. Can I call her?"

"Yes. When we're finished booking you."

"Why do I have to go back to the DMV when I didn't do it? I didn't kill her, I swear."

"DMV? What the hell you talking about? You're in county jail, boy. And from the looks of it, you're gonna be here a while."

And with that, I bend over and puke all over my county-issued shoes.

Willow, OR (KATU)—One suspect has been arrested in connection with the death of 18-year-old Mirabelle Starr, whose body was found early Sunday morning.

Mario Woods, 18, was arrested Monday morning in connection with Starr's death, according to a press release from Stephen Knight, spokesman for the Richland County Sheriff's Office.

Woods had been held in the Richland County jail for contributing to the delinquency of a minor. Meanwhile, detectives were investigating the death and new evidence came to light. "There are investigative details that we're not talking about publicly at this point, including motive and cause of death," Knight said. Woods will make his first court appearance Wednesday at the Richland County Criminal Courthouse.

Starr's body was found in a ditch on Wessinger Road. The girl had gone to prom earlier that night and then to a party hosted by a friend. Her abandoned automobile was found a few miles away from where her body was discovered.

JOSH

No one contacts us. You think they would, right? Maybe they're busy. Maybe they forgot. Or maybe Mirabelle's just another number to them.

So how do we hear about it? From friends and family who see it on the news. Our phone starts ringing Monday around noon. I don't know why we even still have the landline other than Mom doesn't want to get rid of it. I'm still in bed since I hardly slept last night, but the third time it rings, I get up to find out what's going on.

Dead. Dead. Dead.

Not fair. Not fair. Not fair.

Mom turns to me. "Sorry. I'll take it off the hook if you want to try to go back to sleep."

Right. Like there's any way that's gonna happen.

"What's going on?" I ask as I go to the sink to get a drink of water. I fill up my water bottle that's sitting there, then turn around as I take a sip.

"They've arrested that kid you told me about," she says softly. "The one who was prom king. Mario Woods."

Dad's sitting at the table, stone-faced.

"How do they know?" I ask. "Did they say?"

"I bet they got the autopsy results back," Dad says. "And it's possible some good evidence has come to light."

Just then, his phone buzzes. He glances down. "Here we go." When he answers, he says, "Detective, I was wondering when we'd hear from you."

Mom and I don't move. We just stare at him.

"I see," he says.

He listens for a long time. Then he says, "Yes."

There's another long pause. "Okay. And you're certain?" Another pause. "I understand. Thank you. Yes, I will. Goodbye."

He sets his phone back on the table.

This is a nightmare.

We are living in a never-ending nightmare.

"Well?" Mom asks. "What'd he say?"

"We'll get a full report of the autopsy in the next few weeks. In the meantime, the preliminary results are as they suspected. Strangulation. By some kind of object, not by someone's bare hands."

Mom turns to me. "Do you know him? Mario Woods?"

I'm about to answer when Dad says, "You know what? I think he's the kid who took her on a date a couple of years ago in his mom's Mini Cooper. I gave Mir a hard time about it. Do you guys remember that?"

Mom gasps. "*That* was Mario?"

I don't have any recollection of that, but now I'm curious what he looks like and if I know who he is. Could Mario be the reason

I found her sneaking out? "Let me grab my phone and I'll see if I can find him on social media."

I start to move toward my room when I see Mom close her eyes and her face get all crinkly and I can tell she's about to lose it. I go over to her and put my arm around her.

"Why?" she whispers as she leans into my shoulder, crying. "Why would he do it? I don't understand."

"They're probably not going to tell us a thing," Dad says. "We need to be prepared for that. They'll lay out the case in court, though."

I try to imagine that. Going to the courthouse, hearing them talk about my sister, and how he killed her and what led him to do it.

How are we going to do this?

How are we going to get through it?

After a minute, Mom sniffles, wipes her face with her palms and pats my chest before she stands up, straight and tall. "Thanks, Joshy. I'll be okay. I need to get to work. There's a service to plan."

"You doing that today?" I ask. "Already?"

"Yes. We're meeting with the funeral home today and the pastor tomorrow. The service will be Saturday." She looks at me. "No school on Saturday."

"We want everyone who knew her to be able to attend if they want to," Dad explains.

I nod. And then I go to my room to look for Mario Woods online.

MARIO

"Hello, Mario. I'm Jon Bennett, your defense attorney."

Jon's a big guy, like, six-foot-six, at least. Not just tall, but wide too. His coat jacket looks too small. He should probably shop at a big and tall store, but there's nothing like that around here.

I shake his hand before we take a seat at the table in the small room where they've brought me to meet with him. He puts his worn black leather briefcase on the chair next to him and pulls out a yellow pad of paper and a pen.

"How are you doing?" he asks.

I answer with the most honest answer I can. "I want to go home. I hate the food. Hate how cold it is all the time. And my new cellmate? Pretty sure he played linebacker for the Steelers."

"Has he been giving you a hard time?" Jon asks.

"Luckily, no. Can't deny I was scared out of my mind when I saw him. But the first thing he said to me was, 'Don't worry. It's not like you see on TV.' Anyway, this whole thing is a nightmare and I'm glad you're here because I swear, I didn't do it."

"Yeah. I know."

"How do you know?"

He smiles. "'Cause that's what they all say."

"But honestly, I didn't kill her," I say with as much conviction as I can muster.

The thing is, I want him to believe me. No, I *need* him to believe me.

"Look, let me be clear, Mario. Either they found evidence or they have an eyewitness. They might even have both. I know it's difficult, but you need to take this seriously. They wouldn't have arrested you unless they had something on you."

I shake my head. I can't believe this is happening. Just when I think it can't get any worse, it gets worse.

"So what happens next?" I ask.

"On Wednesday, you'll go in front of the judge for the charges being brought against you and for your bond hearing. You'll plead not guilty and we'll request a preliminary hearing. We'll also request bail of a reasonable amount so we can see about getting you out of here while you await your trial at home."

"What are my chances?" I ask. "That I can go home?"

He pulls his legal pad and pen close to him. "Let's not worry about that now. Right now, I need you to tell me your story. Beginning to end. Don't leave a single thing out." He clicks his pen and scribbles in the corner of the pad, making sure it works.

"How do I know if I can, like, trust you?" I ask.

"Everything you tell me will be kept in strict confidence." Then he leans forward slightly. "Mario, think of it this way. Right now? Besides your mother, I'm about the *only* one you can trust. From now on, you only talk to me about your case. No one else. Got it? So when you're ready, let's begin."

PARKER

News spreads through school fast. Of course it does. It's a huge story. Senior guy accused of killing a senior girl on prom night? Not just any guy and girl, either. The freaking prom king and queen of our school.

Most seem shocked by the accusation. I'm sticking with the few who believe he did it. Mario and Belle obviously had some history. And maybe it wasn't all in the past. My stomach twists at the thought. She didn't admit to putting worms in his crown, but I noticed a small paper bag stuffed in her purse earlier that night. I thought she was trying to sneak booze into the dance, but she just laughed when I asked about it. And she didn't give me any other explanation.

The truth is, Mirabelle liked to mess with people. Mostly it was just her joking around—she'd get bored or frustrated or anxious and pull off these elaborate pranks to distract herself. Like when she put that *Playboy* photo in my book. Stupid stuff, innocent. But now I wonder if there was more to it. With the *Playboy*, Belle was pranking me because she liked me. So if she *did* put the worms in Mario's crown . . . is it just further evidence that something was going on between them?

"Hey, Parker," I hear behind me.

I turn from my open locker to find Jason standing there.

"Hey, how's it going?" I ask.

"Rough day, man. I didn't think you'd be here."

"I can't just sit around at home," I tell him. "Grandma checking on me every ten minutes? Trying to get me to eat when my stomach is a mess? No way. I'd go batshit."

"Look, I'm really sorry," Jason says. "I just . . . I wanted you to know that. If there's anything you need . . ."

"Yeah. Thanks." I hesitate for a second, wondering if it's wrong of me to ask him. And then I figure, what the hell do I have to lose. "Did you know anything about her and Mario?"

"What do you mean? I don't think they were involved at all, if that's what you're asking. Though I'm curious, what'd she have to say about that kissing comment on Twitter? You ask her about that?"

"Yeah. I asked on the way to your house. She said they went out once like two years ago, and it was a disaster. I pushed her for more information, but then she shut down. The rest of the night, she barely talked to me. It was bizarre, man."

"You know what else is bizarre?" Jason says. "Mario was with Elana. How could he have committed a crime when she was with him? Like, how is she free if she was there too?"

I grab my notebook and slam the locker door as the second lunch bell rings. "I don't know, but if the evidence shows he did it, I hope they give him the death penalty. Actually, you know what? The more I think about it, the more I wish I could go to the trial and shoot the bastard myself."

Jason and I have calc together, so we start walking that way.

Jason's voice stays soft. Calm. Like he's trying to soothe a wild animal, which just pisses me off more. "Eventually we'll hear about how it all went down. The pieces will come together. It's just hard right now, being in the dark like this."

"But see, that's the thing. I feel like I've been in the dark for a while. Something was going on with her, J. And man, I wish I knew what it was."

"I'm sorry, P." He's already apologized, but I understand there's only so much a person can say. "This is a hell of a lot for you to deal with. You sure you're doing okay? You could skip out early. Pretty sure the teachers would understand."

We stand outside Mr. Phillips's classroom. I think about how I used to see Belle during lunch. How we'd go to her locker and then mine, and we'd kiss goodbye when Jason walked up.

"See ya later?" she'd usually ask.

"Can't wait," I'd say.

Then Jason and I would go to class, just like we are now. Today, I won't be seeing her later. Tomorrow either. Or the next day.

My throat burns and I push the emotions down with every bit of strength I have. Way, way down into a part of myself I didn't even know existed until this happened. Like a deep, dark well that I can't see, but the bucket just keeps dropping farther and farther and farther . . .

My brain whispers to me, *It was all a lie. She never loved you.*

I release the bucket. It drops with a loud clatter.

I'm about to walk into class when Elana walks by. And I explode.

"You little—"

"Leave me alone," she says.

"Did you watch him do it?" I ask, getting right in her face. "Huh? Did you? Let me guess, you got off on it, right? Glad to have one less pretty girl in the world to compete with, yeah?"

Elana starts crying. "Stop. Please."

"Hey," Jason says, pulling me back, away from her. "Come on, man. Leave her alone. We don't have all the pieces yet, remember?"

Elana takes off running down the hall.

"Shit," I mutter as I run my hand through my hair and lean up against the wall. "Maybe I shouldn't be here after all. This is so messed up."

And maybe I have more anger in me than I thought.

I take a deep breath and motion toward class. There's nothing to do but go in and see if calculus can save us from ourselves.

LUCAS

leave school during lunch. When I hear the news about Mario, that he's now their main suspect, I know there's no way I can concentrate after that.

As I unlock my bike in front of the old brick school building that definitely needs a face-lift, I have the same thought I always do when I have to hop on a seat rather than get in a car: I should get a job. It sucks that I only get Mom's car Tuesdays and Thursdays, when Dad takes the twins to school and they stay for the after-school program.

Mario told me a few different times he could try to help me get a job at the Pay-n-Pak if I wanted. We'd joke about whether or not my lazy ass could handle it. But really? It's not a joke. Deep down, I was afraid I couldn't handle it.

I know I need to grow up. But I don't want to. Like, I *really* don't want to. Mom and Dad keep asking me what my plans are for next year. For a long time, I'd just say, "I don't know." Lately, they've pressed me harder, and so I've told them I'm thinking about joining the military. Which is a complete and total lie. I mean, come on. Me? In the military?

After Mario got his college acceptance letter, he said, "You should come too. To Washington. We can be roommates. Don't you want to see my face every day when you wake up and every night before you go to sleep?" I leaned in and pretended to kiss him and we both cracked up so hard.

But the thing is, he's smarter than I am. He has no idea I'm barely passing my classes. I didn't want to tell him there's no way U of W would accept me.

The more I think about Mario, what a good friend he's been to me, the more it feels like I've swallowed sixteen ounces of glass shards. It hurts. It hurts so much.

And just like that, I decide I'm not going home yet.

If the cops aren't going to do the work to find the real killer, then someone else is going to have to do it. Like practically everything else in my sad, sorry life, I don't want to. But who else is there?

I feel the weight of that pressing down on me, and it's so heavy, I want to jump off my bike, sit on the curb and cry. I'm not sure I can handle it, to be honest. Here's the thing, though: every day I go through the motions, pretending like things matter. Telling myself that someday, something will happen and I'll find my purpose in this freaking mess of a world. That I just have to hang on until then.

But there is no pretending with this. Because if anything or anyone matters? It's Mario.

ELANA

After Parker pounced on me and said those horrible things, I ran to the parking lot, jumped in my car and texted Dad that I was going home.

People are saying terrible things.

He texts back: *Canceling my appointments. Be home ASAP.*

The whole way home, I can't stop crying. Once I'm through the door, I go to my room, dump my backpack and tear off my clothes. I slip into my favorite leggings and a long-sleeve tunic. I've always tried to look nice for school. It's seemed so important, for some reason. To look my best. But now? No matter what I do, I can't win. If no one liked me much before, they all hate me now. I'll always be the girl who was with Mario the night Mirabelle was killed. No one around here will ever let me forget it.

Maybe Daddy will let me switch schools. I've always wanted to go to Three Rivers across town. It seems nicer there. I know there isn't much time left before I graduate, but what does it matter? There might be enough time for me to make a new friend or two. This summer I'd have some new people to hang out with. God, I'd love that. And then, in the fall, when I'm off to Otis

College of Art and Design, I'll have some fun memories to take with me. I deserve a good summer before I go away to college.

When I got the acceptance letter from Otis, I was thrilled. First of all, it's in sunny California. Second of all, their fashion design program is one of the best in the country. Third, it's far away from this place. It'll be nice to kind of . . . start over there. No one will know me. Not a soul. I can be whoever I want to be for a change.

I head back downstairs and take a seat in the breakfast nook in the corner of the kitchen. I scroll through IG for a minute but close it out when it's mostly just one photo after another of Mirabelle's locker and totally fake sentiments about how much the poster is going to miss her. Half of those people probably never even said a word to her.

I want to scream at all of them, *Hey, assholes! How about treating people with decency when they're alive instead of waiting until they're dead!*

When Dad walks in, he goes straight to the stove and puts the kettle on.

"You really didn't have to come home," I tell him.

"Elana, I want to be here with you. And thankfully, my patients were very understanding."

"What'd you tell them? That I was an accomplice to a murder and it's really messing with my psyche?"

He turns and stares at me. "Elana. That's not funny. Don't even joke about it. And for the record, I told them you're broken up about the girl who died over the weekend."

"Well, thanks for lying for me, I guess," I say. "But I don't need a babysitter."

"For the love of . . . Sweetheart, I'm worried about you. I should have insisted you stay home after everything that's happened. Although, I had no way of knowing they'd arrest Mario. What happened at school, anyway? Were there reporters there? Did they try to corner you?"

"Nope," I mumble as I pick at one of my toenails. "Just another day of people being jerks because they hate me."

Dad's in the process of pulling two teacups out of the cupboard. I watch his shoulders slump and his head bow as soon as the words are out. I don't know why I do this to him. I know he worries about me. He worries so much.

He turns around and sets the cups on the counter. "You know what? We need to get you in to see Tahni." He pulls his phone out of his pocket.

Tahni's my therapist. And I do not feel like talking to her. All I want to do is curl up on my bed and sleep. Just forget about everything.

"Dad, not today. Please? I'll go tomorrow if you want. But right now, I'm really not up for it." I lean back. "I'm exhausted. I just want to crawl into bed and sleep."

He nods. "All right. I'll call in a little while and set it up." He pauses. "Elana, we need to be realistic here. They could very well call you to the stand to testify. Is there anything you want to tell me?"

I look at him, shocked. "What do you mean by that?"

"Look, I'm trying to stay calm. I really am. But you need to understand something: they wouldn't have arrested him if they didn't have evidence of some kind. Now, I've known Mario's mom for a long time. I want to believe he's a good kid. But who knows?" He stops for a moment. Puts his hand over his mouth, like he doesn't want to say what he's thinking. "Every time I think of him hurting that girl, I realize it could have been you." Tears fill his eyes. "I'm so glad you're okay. That it wasn't you in that ditch."

"Dad, please stop. I'm here. I'm fine."

He turns around and grabs a box of tea bags. "Peach Tranquility okay with you?"

"Yes. But when you said they probably have evidence of some kind, what do you mean? Like, what kind of evidence?"

He puts two tea bags in the cups. "Could be anything. Blood. Hair. Fingerprints. Murder weapon."

Fingerprints?

"Is it possible for me to talk to Mario at all?" I ask. "Could I go down there and see him? I don't really know how jail works."

He gives me a side-eye. "Well, that's a good thing. And I don't either. Let's maybe wait until after his first court appearance. If they let him out on bail, he'll go home and you can talk to him then."

"Wait, what? He could go home?"

"Maybe. Depends on whether or not the judge sees him as a threat to himself or others."

"If his mom needs money, are you going to help her? You know, for the lawyer?"

The kettle starts whistling. He pours the water and brings the teacups to the table. "Well, I've been thinking about that. It's probably best if we stay out of it. I don't want you implicated any more than you already are."

"Implicated? Implicated how?"

"You were with him the entire time, Elana. I know you were joking earlier, but this is serious. If they decide to call you an accomplice, I'm not sure there's much we could do. Even if you say you were sleeping or passed out or whatever, someone could say it's a lie, plain and simple."

"Please don't worry. I don't think that will happen. The cops know I was drinking, and people who drink sometimes pass out." I take the tea bag out and set it on the saucer. It's still too hot to drink.

Dad doesn't wait for his to cool. He just drinks it, grimacing a little as he does. "My job is to protect you. And I will. No matter what. Now, you want anything else? I could make you a sandwich."

"No, I'm good. Thanks."

My phone buzzes. When I check it, I have a Twitter DM from Lucas. His message says: *I need to talk to you. Can you meet me outside Mario's house in like an hour? You know where he lives, right?*

Why does he want to talk to me? I wonder.

I'm not sure my dad will let me leave.

Lucas replies: *It's really important, Elana.*

I can't deny I'm dying to know what he wants. More than I want to watch *Parks and Rec* for the twelfth time, all while hoping I can get my brain to quiet down enough to sleep.

Okay. I'll figure something out. See you soon.

MARIO

've made a decision. A tough one.

While talking to my lawyer, I realized something. If this guy is going to help me, *really* help me, he needs to know what we're up against.

"After you left the party, what'd you do?" Jon asks me.

"Elana didn't want to go home right away. She asked me to drive around for a while. So I did. She was downing those little bottles of alcohol like they were chocolate milk. She'd drink one, throw the bottle out the window, then open another. And look, I should have stopped her. I should have taken them from her and gotten rid of them. I feel really guilty about that."

"Okay. So how long did you drive around?"

"I don't know, man. Who keeps track when you're just killing time, trying to keep the girl next to you happy? All I know is, eventually we came across her along the side of the road."

He cocks his head. "Who's *her*?"

It's not easy, saying her name. In fact, my voice cracks as I say it. "Mirabelle."

He nods slightly and I'm grateful there isn't a stronger reaction. "Okay. What happened next?"

"Her car had broken down. She had the hood up and her flashers on. So I stopped. I got out and she was standing there, sobbing. I offered to look at the car, see if I could get it started, but she didn't want me to. She begged me to give her a ride somewhere."

"Where? Where'd she want to go?"

"To this old half-crumbling barn up the road. She told me someone was gonna meet her there. I asked her three times if she was sure that's what she wanted to do. Because it was getting late, you know?"

"But she said yes?"

I rub my face with my hand. "Yeah. Like I said, that's what she wanted to do. I went to open Elana's door so she could squeeze in with her, but Mirabelle insisted on riding in the bed of the truck. Said we were on a date and she didn't want to ruin it for us."

"What's the bed of your truck like?" Jon asks. He's scribbling notes fast and furious now.

"It has a canopy on it. She's not very big, but I told her she'd still have to slump to be able to sit back there. She said she didn't care. Said she didn't want to inconvenience us any more than she already was."

"If she was in the back," he asks with an eyebrow half-raised, "how did you know where to go?"

"Well, I could have opened the slider window if I needed to talk to her," I explain. "But it wasn't that far. Like, just up the road. She could have walked but, you know . . . heels."

He looks at me kind of funny. "What?"

"She was still dressed for prom. Not exactly easy to walk on a country road dressed like that. Plus, it was dark. Anyway, she told me to turn across the road from a ten-mile-per-hour curve sign. It wasn't hard to find."

"So you pulled up to this barn she insisted on going to. And then what?"

"I got out. Helped her out of the back. She turned on the flashlight on her phone and showed me graffiti on the outside of the barn. Said it was her favorite piece."

"That she had painted?" he asks.

I shrug. "I don't know. I didn't ask. She showed it to me really quickly and then told me to go. Said she didn't want me there when he came."

Now his eyes are stern. Narrow. "When who came?"

"I don't know. She didn't say."

"Didn't you ask? Weren't you curious? Concerned?"

I squeeze my fists and resist the urge to pound them on the table. "Look," I say through gritted teeth, "you weren't there, okay? She seemed completely comfortable." I lean back, take a deep breath, and fold my arms across my chest. "She acted like it was a second home or something. She didn't give me time to ask any questions. She told me to go. Like, she was really pushy about it. Told me to take my beautiful date home, kiss her good night, and not to worry about her. That's what she said, word-for-word pretty much."

He shakes his head, like he's not sure he's hearing me right. "So you just . . . left her there? All by herself? In the dead of night?"

Until now, I've tried my best to push all the guilt down. Bury it. Ignore it. And with everything else going on, it hasn't been too hard. I've been too worried about myself to think much about it. But now? The way he's talking to me? Making me feel like I was stupid for leaving the poor girl there? It's taking everything I have to keep it together.

He's making me see what I've tried to push away. That bright and talented girl is dead because of me. Not because I killed her, but because I didn't take care of her the way I should have. The more I think about it, maybe I deserve to be here. In fact, maybe being charged with Mirabelle Starr's murder is exactly how this should have gone down. Maybe I didn't put my hands on her, but because of my idiotic actions, someone else was able to.

My anger has turned into despair. I haven't let myself feel anything while I've been here, but I can't keep it in any longer. I swallow hard, trying to choke back the tears. "Yeah," I say softly, staring past him because I don't want to see the disgust in his eyes. "I left her there."

"But you didn't go home after that, right?" he says. "Because you found her later."

I want all of this to be over. Can't it just be over? I feel like I could sleep for a week.

"Mario?" he says. "Hey, you okay? You need a break?"

I shake my head as I anxiously crack my knuckles. "Nah. Let's finish this." I sit up straight and look at him. I talk fast. "After we dropped Mirabelle off at the barn, Elana asked if we could get something to eat. She said her stomach was a little upset. So we went to the Little Country Store. You know where that is, right? We got some snacks and some 7UP, ate in my truck. When we finished, she said I should take her home. I turned on some soft music, Elana got sleepy and curled up in the seat. I hadn't gone far when I spotted the body."

"So how much time was that? Since you'd last seen Mirabelle?"

"Um, I don't know. Thirty minutes, maybe?" My mind drifts back to the moment I saw her. Dead. I didn't want it to be true. "When I saw something in the ditch, I pulled over. Just like I told the cops. Got out. And then the deputy showed up a minute later."

"You didn't wake Elana?"

I shake my head. "No. There wasn't really time."

"So how much of this did you tell the police?" he asks.

I stare at the table in front of me. "I didn't tell them I saw Mirabelle at all after the party. I told them we drove around for an hour and then I spotted her body."

"I haven't spoken to the detectives or the district attorney or anyone yet," he tells me. "I'm going to do that soon. Are you telling me that they don't know any of this? That you gave her a ride? That you left her at the old barn alone? That you went to the store and got something to eat?"

"Right. I didn't tell them any of that." I gulp. "I was afraid, okay? I thought it would make me look bad. I mean, I was one of the last ones to see her alive, you know?"

"It's all right. I understand. You didn't have to tell them anything, really. I'm guessing they arrested you because they found prints or something in your truck." He leans in. "But there's something you just told me that might help your case, young man."

151

"Huh? What do you mean?"

"If we can get the clerk at the Little Country Store who was working that night to make a statement regarding the approximate time you were there, that could help you."

I blink a few times. Oh, my god. Why didn't I think of that? "You really think so? You think we have a chance?"

"All we can do is try. I'll get to work on this right away. If it goes the way we want, it could really put a hole in the prosecutor's case."

A hole is good, I guess, although a cavern would be even better.

JOSH

'm in my room, listening to music, trying to help Mom choose the songs to play at Mirabelle's service.

Dead.

My sister is dead.

How is this my life right now?

Someone knocks.

"Come in."

I take my headphones off just as a guy I vaguely recognize appears. He talks quickly. "Hey, Josh. Sorry to bother you. Um, your mom said it was okay to talk to you for a few minutes."

"Am I supposed to know you?" I ask.

He cringes. "Man, I'm sorry. I'm Lucas. I'm a senior. Like your sister. Obviously." He cringes even more before he says, "I didn't know her very well, but, uh, wow, she was a really amazing girl and I'm so sorry for your loss."

"Thanks. So. You need something?"

He quietly shuts the door and approaches my desk, where I'm sitting. When he speaks, he lowers his voice. "Look, I'm here because I need your help. Your parents just think I'm here to give my condolences. But there's more. The cops are doing a crappy job of investigating this case."

"Why do you say that?" I ask as I get up and take a seat on my bed. I motion for him to take my chair, so he does. While he sits, I notice his hands are shaking. And perspiration covers his face. Just as I'm wondering how he can stand it, he pulls a red-and-white bandanna from his pocket and wipes his forehead with it.

"I say that because they have the wrong guy," he says. "There's no way Mario would do something like this. Trust me. I've known him a long time. He's the first person to help someone, not hurt them."

"But they must have something on him, right? Otherwise, they wouldn't have arrested him."

"Maybe. But I really want to do some asking around on my own. I thought you might be willing to tell me what you know about that night."

"Not much, really. None of us heard her leave again after Parker dropped her off. Probably because we've got the busy road right off our neighborhood, and she parks her car on the street. Anyway, as far as we can tell, she pretended to come inside but as soon as Parker left, she got in her car and took off. No clue where she was going." I pause. "There is something you might not know, though."

His eyes narrow. "What?"

"Parker's grandma told us Mirabelle broke up with Parker after the prom."

"Whoa. Seriously?"

"That's what she said. And she has no reason to lie, right? I keep wondering if maybe Mirabelle had found someone else. She was sneaking out sometimes. I caught her once. And I overheard her on the phone with someone the night before she died. They were planning to meet up and . . . I'm not really sure. Honestly, it sounded like maybe they were up to something. I don't know what was going on with her. She was gonna tell me, but she never got the chance." As soon as it's out, I wonder if I shouldn't have said that. "No one knows any of this, by the way. I probably should have told the detectives, but . . . I don't know what she'd want. If she was doing something illegal, is it even worth mentioning? It feels like it matters now more than ever—protecting her."

Lucas leans back and takes a deep breath. "Did they find her phone? Because Christ on a bike, if she had a secret boyfriend or something, that changes everything. Right?"

"They haven't found it," I tell him. "The cops said so. But I bet they can request her phone records, don't you think?"

Lucas pulls out his phone. "What about social media?" he asks. "Does she have an Instagram account?"

"Not sure, to be honest," I say. "I don't have one, so I wouldn't know."

"Did she ever send you any pictures that seemed unusual?" Lucas asks.

"Like, how so?"

"I don't know. Anything that seemed different somehow?"

"Not that I can think of."

Lucas pulls up Instagram and is tapping around on it. "I think I found it. Her username was MiracleBaby. But it's set to private. Any idea what her password might be?"

I look down at my hands before I meet his eyes again. "You swear you're not gonna do anything to hurt her? Or us?"

"I swear, Josh. I just want to find out the truth."

"Try salamander9999. Just a guess, but it's one our family uses for Netflix and stuff."

"Yep. That's it." He stands up. "Thanks, man. I need to go. I'm meeting someone in a little while, and it's important."

"Can you let me know if you find anything?"

"Sure. What's your number?"

After we exchange numbers, Lucas tells me, "If you think of something that might help me find out who she was seeing, let me know, okay?"

"Yeah. I will."

"I really appreciate your help, Josh. I mean it."

"Well, we want the truth too, you know?"

"Yeah. I know. See ya later."

After he leaves, I download Instagram and pull up Mirabelle's account so I can see what she's posted.

I scroll through her photos, expecting to find mostly ones of her and Parker. But that's not what I find. Not even close.

ZAIN

When I met Mirabelle, it was like Vizie's Smiley Face yellow.

Like sunshine for days.

She wanted to join us, to become a painter in the dark. How could we refuse?

And so we got to be friends. That's all. Friends. For almost a year. Until suddenly, a month or so ago . . . we became more. We didn't mean for it to happen. Maybe that's what they all say. But it's true.

There was a Logic concert. Mir loved him. But her prickhead of a boyfriend hated rap music. So we went with her. She told her family a new friend from school had invited her to go.

A new friend? A NEW FRIEND?! Ecstatic. That's what they were. Didn't question it. As for Parker, she told him a different story. *Need to study for an exam. Don't text. Don't call. Too hard to concentrate.*

So there we were. Our little crew. Happy. Free. Energized. Like Midnight Blue outlined with Punk Pink. We pulled over to get some gas. Mir and I went into the mini-mart. Had a funny argument about what kind of doughnuts to get. I wanted choco-late, she wanted powdered sugar. "Could you be any whiter?" I teased.

The place smelled like old coffee and hot dogs. Nothing ro-mantic about it at all. But it didn't matter. She was smiling and shit, and my heart, my Strawberries&Cream Red heart, couldn't take it anymore. I pulled her close to me and I kissed her.

Felt like the bravest thing I'd ever done. She could have pushed me away. Should have pushed me away. Boyfriend, off scene. Don't forget. I never forgot. Trust me. But that's not what happened. Not even close. She leaned in to me, and as I tasted her sweet, sweet lips, the ugly mini-mart faded away. Just me and her and the hope of something good and right and true.

When we pulled away, she said, "I've been waiting for you to do that."

I laughed. "You kidding me?"

"No," she said as she took my hand and wove her fingers with mine. I loved the picture of that. "I've never been more serious, actually."

"But you and Parker," I tried to explain.

She anxiously brushed her long bangs out of her face. "I know, I know," she whispered. "Except I want to be with you. The truth is . . ." She stared awkwardly at her shoes for a second before she looked at me again. "I can't stop thinking about you."

When she said it, it felt like the floor was falling out be-neath me.

Dropping.

Falling.

Exhilarating.

Terrifying.

Before I could say something, a group of girls barged through the door. Talking and laughing. Our mini-mart moment was over. She grabbed the doughnuts, two of each kind, along with a couple of sodas, while I grabbed some batteries for our head-lamps before we headed to the counter to pay. Our usual haul.

Back outside, she put her finger to her lips and mouthed, "Our secret, okay?"

And just like that, the euphoria I'd felt just two short minutes before evaporated into thin air. *You wanna keep this a secret? Keep us a secret? Hold on. You're asking me to pretend I don't have these crazy intense feelings thrumming through me?*

What the hell?

How?

But we found our way. Texted constantly, day and night. Snuck out. Met up late at night. While everyone else dreamed in monochrome, Mir and I lived in Technicolor.

Late-night movies. Skittles for her. Licorice for me. Making out. Walks in the rain. Making out. Swinging in the park. Making out. Driving through town with the music loud. Making out. Sharing secrets. Sharing dreams. Making out.

Eventually, we told Harry and Shannon, who'd also hooked up somewhere along the way. Went from four friends to two couples and, god, those nights we were all out together, paint-ing the world with our hearts and our cans, were some kind of magical.

Now, when I pull up to the old half-standing barn that sits

on abandoned property where we sprayed yellow-and-black sunflowers, it feels like I'm gonna liquid scream.

She'll never be here again.

I'll never see her again.

Ever.

ELANA

park down the street because there are television crews in front of Mario's house. I'm guessing that Lucas didn't think about this possibility when he made Mario's house our meeting spot. I feel bad for his mom, having to deal with all this.

After my mom left us, Ms. Woods came over sometimes after work and helped us with stuff around the house. She brought us food, did the dishes, folded laundry, cleaned the bathroom. Dad and I could have done that stuff, of course. It's not like we didn't help when Mom was around. But I think Ms. Woods knew we were in shock, and just doing the basics to get through the day was hard enough.

Ms. Woods was a godsend; that's what Daddy said. Eventually, he hired a housekeeper for us, but those early days? We needed someone, and Ms. Woods was there for us in a big way.

As time went on, she stopped by less and less. I was really surprised to see her one day a couple of months later, when my dad wasn't even home. He usually texted me on his way out the door. I hadn't received a text from him yet, and I'd invited a guy from the other high school over to "study." We'd met at an art camp that summer and I really liked him.

When Ms. Woods knocked on the door, it scared the shit out of us. We were making out, right there on the couch, which she could easily see from the front window. I jumped up, straightened myself out and opened the door.

She looked from me to the boy and back to me again. "I'm sorry to, uh, interrupt," Ms. Woods said. "But your dad is working late tonight. Got an emergency walk-in a few minutes ago. I offered to take you out to dinner, since I haven't seen you in a long time. What do you say?"

"I should go," the guy said as he got up and grabbed his backpack. "I didn't realize it was so late." I never heard from him again after that. I wish I had. I even found his socials and tried messaging him, but they all went unread.

Ms. Woods ended up taking me out for Chinese food and didn't say a thing about what she'd seen. Mostly, we compared notes on our favorite Netflix shows. When she brought me home, she asked, "Are you doing okay, sweetie?"

"Hanging in there, I guess," I told her.

"School going all right?"

"When you're the one kids love to hate? Sure, fantastic!" As soon as it was out, I regretted it. No one wants to hear stuff like that.

Pity practically poured out of her eyes. "Oh, Elana. You have friends to support you though, right? I mean, it's not all bad, is it?"

What was I supposed to say? That I'm a big loser? A loner who keeps to herself because that's much easier than being bullied and rejected over and over again? I mean, jeez, my own mother rejected me. But Ms. Woods didn't want to hear any of that. And even if she did, I knew there wasn't anything she could do about it.

I gave her my best "everything's fine" smile. "Sorry. Sometimes my sense of humor is a little twisted. Please don't worry. I have some good friends and everything's fine."

"Glad to hear it," she said before she reached over and gave me an awkward hug, right there in the car.

I about jump out of my skin when there's a knock on my car window, interrupting my thoughts. I turn to find a sweaty face staring at me.

I roll down my window. "What the hell? You scared the crap out of me."

"Sorry."

I motion to the news vans. "Can you believe this?"

"No," Lucas says, turning to look. "His poor mom. Like it's not bad enough her son is in jail, now she has to deal with freaking-nosy-as-hell reporters."

"So . . . you want to get in or what?" I ask.

"Oh. Uh . . . okay. I guess. Sure."

He runs around and hops into the front seat. "Thanks for meeting me. What'd you tell your dad?"

"I told him I needed to go see a friend who's really broken up about Mirabelle's death. He could hardly say no to that. What do you want, anyway?"

"I want to hear your side of the story," he tells me. "The thing is, I know Mario. There's no way he did what they're saying he did. But it seems like the cops have already made up their minds. I just want to see if there are any other possibilities."

I sigh. "Look, I told everything to the detectives. I was passed out in the front seat. I don't remember anything. I know that's not what you want to hear, but that's all I've got. There's really nothing I can do to help him. I'm sorry."

"So you had too much to drink?" he asks.

"Yes. Obviously. That's why I passed out and why he was arrested in the first place."

"They gave you a Breathalyzer test?"

"Yes. At the scene. They gave him one too, but he hadn't been drinking."

He leans back in the seat and closes his eyes.

When he doesn't move, I clear my throat. "Sorry, but I need to get back home. My dad will be worried if I'm gone too long. He's pretty freaked out about everything. As you can imagine."

Lucas sits up straight. His eyes are filled with concern. "Are you sure there's nothing you can think of that might help Mario? Please, Elana. Isn't there anything?"

He's desperate. I get it. His best friend is in jail. And he's innocent. I know it and he knows it. But this is beyond us. We're just two kids.

"No. There isn't," I tell him. "You should probably admit that this thing is out of our hands."

"Bullshit," he yells as he slams his hand on the dash.

"Hey." I'm done being nice. "You need to go, okay? I cooperated with the police. I think you should let them do their jobs. They're the experts, you know?"

"Elana . . ."

"Get out, Lucas." He stares at me. "Now!"

That does it. He hurries out of the car like a frightened kitten being chased by a German shepherd.

Once he's shut the door, I speed away from the news cameras, hoping they don't decide to come visit me next. If they do, too bad. They're not getting anything out of me.

LUCAS

When I get home, I tell Mom I'm tired and I need to lie down. She doesn't question it. She sells Mary Kay, so she works from home, though it's about time for her to go and pick up my younger twin sisters from school. Once they're home, she'll mostly forget about me, like always. Unless I try to go to the kitchen and get myself something to eat. These days, I keep a stash of food in my room, though.

I get into Mirabelle's IG account to look for clues. The most recent photo she posted was of her in her prom dress. She took it standing in front of a full-length mirror. She looked gorgeous. Like, whoa. Never seen her dressed up like that. It's something else.

The photo before that one was a week ago. It's the word *love* painted on a wall of some kind. It doesn't look familiar. The art is big, bright and beautiful, with every color of the rainbow in there. She captioned it *How do you know if you've found it?*

I read through the thirty replies. Carefully. Methodically. A whole bunch of emoji responses. A few: *You just know.* One: *Your heart won't lie.* One: *The universe will let you know somehow.* And one: *The more you try to deny it, the more your heart screams at you.*

That one stands out because she didn't say she was denying it. Not even close. I click on the name and find an account filled with graffiti. But not just the finished art; actual graffiti in process. It looks like this account is owned by a crew of artists. Some of the posts feature the painters. One of them makes me gasp out loud.

I can't see her face, but I can see her small silhouette and her long blond hair.

It's Mirabelle. I know it is. But who, exactly, are the people she's with?

ZAIN

On Monday evening, Harry finds me at our spot. Staring. Staring at one of our crew's best pieces with tears streaming down my cheeks.

I hear him slam the door on his old VW van. It's given our crew so many good times. All that feels like a distant memory now.

The air is cool and tinged with a sweet woody smell. I reach up. Swipe at my face. If only you could wipe away grief that easily.

Harry stands next to me. "We should add a tag with her dates. That's what they do with the angels, right?"

"Was just thinking that," I say. "Want to do it now?"

He shrugs. "Might as well."

I turn to him. "You think he did it? Parker? You think he killed her? She told me she was going to break up with him. Finally."

"Are you sure she actually did it, though? I mean, hadn't she told you she was gonna do that, like, ten times at least? Besides, they arrested that other kid. Mario, I think."

The wind picks up.

"I don't know. . . . I just have this feeling. She promised me,"

I say. "Last week I tried breaking it off with her and she wouldn't let me. She said she'd do it. Said she'd break up with Parker so we could be together for real."

"I honestly thought you guys were done."

"I know. But then it felt like I should give her one last chance. And now . . ."

"When was the last time you talked to her?"

I sniffle. "She texted on prom night. From her latest burner. Said she wanted to see me. Had something to tell me. And I tried to get to her, but my parents had friends over and they refused to go home. No way Ma was gonna let me leave after one in the morning, and it was too damn hard to sneak out. I asked Mir to just tell me over the phone or something, but she said she wanted to do it in person. Last thing I said to her was, 'Not gonna make it. I'm really sorry. I tried. Maybe tomorrow night?' All she said back was 'Okay.'"

"You think she was gonna tell you she broke up with him?"

"I don't know. I want to believe that's what it was, but I just don't know."

A lonely train whistle, deep and sorrowful, calls out in the darkness. I imagine hopping on and riding somewhere far, far away.

"Maybe it wasn't good news," Harry tells me. "It was prom. Something could have happened to change her mind, you know?"

It's just about pitch-black out now. I try to hide the anger in my voice. "What are you trying to do, man?"

"I'm trying to say there are different scenarios here, Z. Maybe it was about to be over for you guys. And if so, doesn't that help it hurt a little less?"

"No," I say. "Either way, she's gone. Either way, my heart is cracked wide open. Either way, and I swear to god this is true, I loved her."

————

A little while later, my hands move across the spot at the bottom of the wall. White spray paint speckles my dark brown skin. I paint her name, or the one she went by with us, anyway—Miracle. Then Harry paints her birth date. And stops.

"What date should I put?" he asks.

I pull out my phone to double-check. "May fifteenth."

He finishes it off. Stands back. Turns. The damn headlamp shines right in my eyes.

"Light, man!"

"Sorry. You want to add anything?"

I go up nice and close so I can see it. "Nah. Looks good."

After we turn off our headlamps, darkness overtakes us again. Guessing that's what the coming days and weeks will feel like—brief periods of light swallowed up by overwhelming darkness.

"She was quite the girl," Harry says.

I remember the way she laughed and how there was not a sound I loved more.

I remember the way she rubbed my hand with her thumb and how it sent shivers down my spine. Every. Single. Time.

I remember how I wanted her all to myself, and the longer I went on having to "share" her, the more miserable I became.

She was Raspberryripple Purple. I was Neverland Teal. We belonged together. A perfect pair.

"Gonna miss her so damn much," I say softly.

"I know" is all Harry says. Because what else can you say, really?

MARIO

When I get back to my cell, my cellmate is reading a book. Maybe he can see it in my face that I don't feel like talking. I climb onto my cot and roll toward the wall. The last place I should probably be is alone with my thoughts, but talking to a probable felon isn't exactly a good option either. Over the last eighteen hours I've swung from depressed to pissed off to sad to scared shitless, and everything in between. The one thing that's remained, however, is the immense guilt I feel.

For letting Elana drink too much.

For leaving Mirabelle at the barn.

For not thinking everything through better when it really counted.

I pound the wall with my fist. Hard.

A girl who had her whole life ahead of her is dead. Her family has lost a daughter and a sister. Kids at school have lost a friend.

And then there's my family. It's just my mom and me, and if my mom loses me, it'll devastate her. I hope she has someone helping her through right now. It makes me sick to my stomach, thinking of her losing sleep over this. Over me. Jon had me fill out a visitor request form and he said he'd get her in to see me tomorrow. It'll be on a phone, through a glass window, like I've seen on TV, but it's better than nothing. It's insane to think about the fact that society now views me as a hardcore criminal. I'm not a hardcore anything. Wait, let me think on that a minute.

Hardcore mango eater?

Hardcore *Battlestar Galactica* fan?

Hardcore cat-video watcher?

At least Jon the attorney dude gave me a sliver of hope. Will the guy at the Little Country Store remember me? Will the investigators listen to the new evidence presented? Will they be convinced enough to let me out of here? Let me go home, where I belong?

What will they say when they hear I lied to them in my statement at the scene? They could be pissed at me for not telling them the truth, even if I had good reasons for doing so. Shit. I thought if I told them I saw Mirabelle that night and gave her a ride, it'd make me look even guiltier.

I don't want to believe that they would let things stand only to see me punished for my stupidity. But anything is possible. I know that as sure as I know I'm sitting in this cold, ugly jail cell. I hope Jon plays the "stupid young kid" card—as in, tells them I didn't know any better.

All I can do is wait and see. And pray the sliver of hope grows a little brighter with every passing hour.

ZAIN

Mir wrote me a letter after I almost broke up with her. An actual letter, on lemon-yellow stationery with gold accents she picked out herself. Did she buy just one sheet? Or a whole tablet to have on hand whenever she felt the urge to write, pen on paper?

She was always bugging me to get online. Wanted me to read her fan fiction. I just wasn't interested. Wish I had been. Guess I still can. Pretty sure I'll be her biggest fan.

When I got the letter, I was confused at first. But then? At the end? It all made sense. And how could I not grant her wish? To do it in her own time, in her own way?

Monday morning, after tossing and turning all night, I pull out the letter. I read it again.

Dear Zain,

Dreary.
Dingy.
Suffocating.
Those are just a few of the adjectives that
come to mind when I think of this hellhole we live
in. Nothing to do but find a backseat and make
out. Nothing to see but the used-car lot, the
Dollar Tree, and the Hasty Freeze. Nothing to hear
but the sound of dreams being buried alive.
   I knew of you before I met you, you know.
   They called you vandals.
   Rebels.
   Thieves of All That Is Sacred.
   I called you creators.
   Artists.
   Donors of All That Is Beautiful.
   When I discovered the "Believe" piece on the
crumbling wall behind the Little Country Store,
that was when I knew I had to meet you and your
crew. The yellow sun emerging from behind the
bright blue letters—it filled me with something I
hadn't felt since I was five and saw an ice cream
truck for the very first time.
   Goodness.
   Hope.
   Possibility.

175

I was so happy when I found you weeks later, on a warm, starlit June night almost a year ago, painting the town hopeful. You were working on that piece under the old wooden bridge. Remember? A book open to a page that says, "Knowledge is freedom."

"Can I join you?" I asked.

"Why?" you asked me. "Why do you want to?"

"Honestly?" I said. "If I don't do something, I'm afraid I'll shrivel up and die. I need this. I need to feel the hope from the arteries of my tiny, fearful heart all the way to the very tips of my fingers. Please?"

Little did I know that weeks later, I would need the promise of hope more than I could have ever imagined. When Josh was diagnosed with leukemia, it felt like I was the one who was going to die. Lucky for me, the three of you let me in. And my life was forever changed.

Zain, if people knew about us, they would say terrible things. They'd call me a cheater, a slut, a heartless bitch. The thing is, I know it's wrong. I know I should've broken up with Parker as soon as it began. But breaking hearts is not something I enjoy doing. And believe me, it will break his heart.

Mostly, I want you to know that in the end, I am the crumbling wall and you are the spray can.

We belong together, that I know for sure. And one day we will be a masterpiece unlike anything the world has ever seen.

But sometimes greatness takes time. So please, give me a little bit more. I'm going to do it. Soon. And then you'll see, the waiting will have been worth it. I promise.

My heart is yours,
Mirabelle

JOSH

Mirabelle's IG account is a combination of books, sunsets and graffiti. Some of the graffiti I've seen before around town and some of it I haven't. I know she loved art of any kind, and now, after seeing all this, I'm guessing that's what she was talking about on the phone that night. She was gonna meet up with someone and paint graffiti.

She has a shitload of followers. Like, over a thousand. The only thing I can figure is that she gave her handle out to some of the people who followed her fan fiction online. Unless people who do graffiti advertise it secretly somehow and gain supporters.

The fact that she wrote fan fiction and shared it with the world proves she wasn't afraid of the hate you get online sometimes. So the only reason she'd make this account private is to keep her family and friends from knowing what she was doing.

She was obviously hiding something from us. But is the graffiti the only thing? That's what I can't stop thinking about. I keep trying to recall other things that might have been clues. Things she said or did. But nothing comes up.

When Mom told me we all needed to work together to prepare Mirabelle's memorial service, she told me brain fog is normal when you're in a state of grief.

Foggy? My brain is like a category five hurricane right about now.

There's a knock followed by, "Josh? Can I come in?"

"Yeah." I close out of Mirabelle's account and put my phone facedown on my bed.

"Hey," Mom says. She looks like she hasn't slept in months. Hard to believe it's only been two nights.

Not fair. Not fair. Not fair.

She comes over and sits on my bed. "Wanted you to know there are reporters outside. I'm guessing they want to know what we think of Mario being arrested."

"That's so stupid," I say. "What we want is justice for Mirabelle. If he did it, and they prove it, then justice is served."

Mom nods. "Yes, but they may have found out Mario and Mir were prom king and queen. Drama makes for good headlines. They may be hoping for more of a story from us."

"Well, I won't say anything. Don't worry."

"I'm not worried. I just wanted you to know, that's all."

"We don't even have to go out there, do we?" I ask. "I mean, it's not like we need to go anywhere. Seems like we have enough food for days."

"Hmm," she says. "This is true. Pastor McCarthy is coming here this afternoon, though. I hope they don't make the poor guy push his way through the crowd to get to our front door."

It's quiet for a moment.

"Mom?"

"Yeah?"

"How are we going to get through it. The service, I mean?"

She takes a deep breath as she stares out my window looking out into the backyard. I can see the big tree with the tree house from here. When Dad and I first built it years ago, Mirabelle and I fought over who got to use it. Then one night at dinner, she put her finger up in the air and said, "I know what we need to do, Josh. We'll make a schedule. Something like Mondays, Wednesdays and Fridays, you can use it, and Tuesdays, Thursdays and Saturdays, I can use it. That's fair, right?"

"What about Sundays?" I asked.

"Sundays, we share," she stated matter-of-factly.

The first Sunday, one of those perfect summer afternoons where it's not too hot with a nice breeze blowing, we sat up there reading books. She wanted to play music. I wanted it to be quiet. She let it be quiet. When it was time to go in for dinner, she put her arm around my shoulders on the way inside. "You know what? It's not so bad sharing with you."

I wanted to tell her if I had my way, we'd share all the time. I hadn't wanted it all to myself. Not really. I'd just wanted her to include me when she wanted to use it. But she was older and little brothers are annoying. But as for me? I adored my big sister. Big time.

Now, Mom turns and looks at me. "I'm taking Xanax when I need to. It helps. If you want, I can see if the doctor can prescribe something for you as well. It makes me feel calm. Not as anxious.

If I take a higher dose, which my doctor said I could do for a while, it even puts me to sleep."

"So are you saying you plan on sleeping through the service?" I'm only joking. And fortunately, she seems to know that because she smiles just slightly.

"Nope. Can't do that. I gotta say goodbye to my baby girl, Joshy. Don't want to be asleep for that." Her bottom lip trembles. "I can't believe how much I miss her."

I sit up and hug her. Does it take the pain away, even for a second? I can only hope.

Funny how the feeling of missing isn't really something missing at all.

PARKER

When I get home Monday night, reporters are waiting for me. Grandma texted me and warned me. Looks like the story has blown up and gone national. I guess it makes sense. A girl murdered on prom night makes for a good story. Pretty sure *People* magazine lives for headlines like that.

PROM KING KILLS PROM QUEEN IN A FIT OF RAGE!

I told Grandma I could handle them. The media. We live close to the school, so I either walk or ride my bike. This morning I felt like walking. Now I'm wishing I'd ridden my bike so I could just plow into anyone who gets in my way.

They rush up to me when they spot me and start shouting questions.

"Parker, what do you think of Mario being arrested?"

"Do you think he did it because of what she said on Twitter?"

"Do you think something more had been going on between them?"

I don't know what makes me do it. I could say it's the voice in my head that won't shut up, but that makes me sound insane. And I'm not insane. Am I?

I stop and look around. The cameras are running. The microphones are frozen midair, all of them hoping I'll give them something juicy. Ratings. That's all they want. All they care about. But what about me? What about what *I* care about? What *I* want?

"I want everyone to know one thing. Mirabelle was an amazing person. I wish you all could have known her. She was a writer. An artist. An actress. She loved the ocean. She loved sea lions and dolphins and manatees, and she wanted to try to make the world a better place for them. She had a good heart, you know?" I swallow hard. "I don't know why anyone would want to kill someone like that. All I know is a wonderful human is gone. And every day she's not here is a sad day. And that's all I really have to say."

They shout more questions at me, but I rush to the front door and get inside as fast as I can. Grandma turns from the front window, where she was watching me.

"What'd you say to them?" she asks.

"Basically? That she was a great girl. And my heart is broken."

And then I go upstairs to my room.

Donny: This day was depressing af.

Jason: Right? Can't believe Parker came to school today.

Donny: He looked like shit.

Jason: He told me something. I don't think many people know.

Donny: What? What'd he say?

Jason: Mir broke up with him. After they left my place. Whoever killed her did it after that.

Donny: Whoa

Jason: Right?

Donny: I've been thinking. Mario doesn't seem like the type. You know?

Jason: Yeah. I know. What a clusterfuck.

Donny: You okay man?

Jason: It just

Donny: What?

Jason: It sucks. That's all. The whole thing sucks.

185

JANICE WOODS

Carol came over and spent the day with me. It was so kind of her. I don't know what I would have done without her. When the attorney came to see me, gave me the form to fill out so I could go see Mario tomorrow, I almost cried right there on the spot. Partly from relief and partly from the fear I've been carrying around like a bag of bricks. At some point, the bag's gotta break.

"Is he doing okay?" I asked him.

"He seems to be, yes."

"I'm so worried about him."

"I know. But he really is doing fine."

Jon went over some things with me, and then he was off to turn in the paperwork so I could be approved for a visit.

After he left, my dear friend was right there, ready to offer up a shoulder. Once I got it together, I called Dr. Dexter and told him I'd need another day off. He told me to take the entire week off, that they could manage without me for five short days. In some ways, it might be good to get back to work and keep my racing mind occupied.

When Carol arrived this morning, she brought some more

food for me along with a jigsaw puzzle and a couple of paperback books from her own shelves. Even she knows I need to try to stay busy. Easier said than done, but I know I should try.

As I'm hunting for the edge pieces on a puzzle of two kittens, the landline rings.

"Hello?"

"Hello, Ms. Woods? This is Elana."

"Oh, Elana. How nice to hear from you."

"Are you . . . doing okay? I mean, I know you're probably anxious. About Mario. But . . . are you, like, okay?"

"Yes. I'm all right. Thank you for asking. It's very sweet of you to check on me. How are you?"

"I'm worried too. I tried to go to school today but it was horrible. Dad came home early so I wouldn't be alone. I mean, I told him he didn't have to stay with me, but he wanted to."

"I'm glad he did."

"Um, I was wondering, do you get to see him at all? Mario?"

"As a matter of fact, I'll be going tomorrow."

"Oh. Okay. If I wrote him a letter, do you think you could pass it on to him? Would that be all right? I just want to tell him how sorry I am about all this. He's such a nice guy and he really doesn't deserve this. Would you mind?"

"I'm not sure how things work, if I'll be able to give him anything, but I'm happy to try."

"Okay, thanks. I can drop it by in the morning. What time are you going?"

"I haven't heard yet. Why don't you come by around ten? I don't expect it will be before that."

"Okay, I'll come then. Thanks so much."

"No problem. Do you remember how to get here?"

"Yeah. See you tomorrow."

"All right, sweetie. Good night."

"Night."

It'll be good for Mario to know he has people out here thinking about him. Hoping for the best. I know Lucas is worried sick as well. At least Mario's attorney seems invested in the case. He seems to have Mario's best interest at heart. As far as I can tell, anyway.

When I spoke with Jon, he told me not to despair. That something had emerged he couldn't speak about yet, but he felt optimistic about the case.

I'm holding on to that thought, even though it's hard. I hope Mario is too.

LUCAS

'␣ve never done anything like this. Snuck out to meet strangers. But I have to see if I can find them. I just have to.

From what I can tell, the crew is from the other high school. There was a picture of the three of them, without Mirabelle, outside the Taco Time across town. I couldn't find any real names, just made-up ones—their tag names or whatever they're called. I think that's where her username, MiracleBaby, came from. Her tag was Miracle. The others are Zen, Prince and Red.

I scoot into the driver's seat of Mom's car and gently close the door. I never thought I'd say this, but right now, I'm loving the fact that she drives a Prius. It's making my life a whole lot easier. It's pretty amazing how quiet the thing is; I can slide out of the driveway and no one's the wiser. The first time I rode in it and Mom stopped at a stoplight, I thought the engine had died.

I drive around town looking for that green VW van, but I don't see it. I decide they probably do more of their work away from town. So I drive out along the country roads, but it starts to feel like searching for a thumbtack in a bucket of nails. Do I think I'm just going to stumble upon them spray-painting a wall somewhere?

It's hard to imagine Mirabelle sneaking out, living a double life that no one knew about. Meeting up with friends carrying backpacks of spray cans, hoping to share a little art with the world. I wonder what that felt like? Frightening? Exciting? Probably both. Exhilarating. I bet that's what it was, even if I've never experienced it myself.

As I head home, I realize there's a better way to find them. I know what the van looks like. And the van is probably parked in the parking lot of Three Rivers High every day.

Looks like I'll be leaving school a little early again tomorrow.

ELANA

On Tuesday morning, I drop the letter off for Ms. Woods to take to Mario, and then head to my appointment with Tahni. I've been seeing her for years. Her office is located on the second floor of an old building downtown. Downtown makes it sound so fancy, but in Willow, downtown means Main Street with shops, a couple of diner-type restaurants and some professional businesses. It takes all of five minutes to walk from one end to the other.

When I get to her office, Tahni calls me in and offers me a cup of tea. She's done that ever since she discovered I'm an avid tea drinker. She always has good flavors, so I say, "Sure. Thanks."

I take a seat on the purple sofa. Her office is as colorful as a box of crayons. Purple sofa, red chairs, butter-yellow walls, dark blue bookcases.

When she hands me the mug, she says, "When I heard the news, I wondered if I might hear from you this week." She sits in her comfy chair across from me. "Did you know her very well? Mirabelle?"

"Not really," I say. I blow on the hot water, trying to cool it down.

"Still pretty shocking, huh?"

"Yeah. And you know the guy they've arrested? Mario Woods?"

"Yes?"

"I went to prom with him."

Tahni is one of those people who can raise one eyebrow really high. Just one. I've tried to do it so many times, but apparently I don't have that special talent. Every session, it's like a challenge to see if I can say something that will make her do it. When she does it now, I can't help but smile ever-so-slightly.

"Wait. Am I hearing you right, Elana? Your prom date is the person they've arrested in connection with her murder?"

I nod as I sip my tea. I'm sure there are a million questions she wants to ask me now. I wait to see which one she'll choose.

"So tell me what happened. From your perspective."

"From my perspective? Um, okay. Well, Mirabelle was in a ditch. Dead. Mario saw her as he was driving by, so he stopped. A deputy came by, and I guess that looked pretty suspicious. They don't have any better suspects, so they're pinning it on him, basically."

She narrows her eyes. "But you were with him. Weren't you?"

I don't want to answer this question anymore. I'm tired of it. Tired of feeling ashamed and regretful and a hundred other things. "I, um, passed out. Had a little too much to drink."

"They think he killed her with you passed out in the car? That'd be pretty bold, wouldn't it?"

I take a swig of tea and then set the mug down on the small table at the end of the sofa. "I don't know what they think, to be honest. All I know is they let me go and they arrested him."

"How does that make you feel, Elana?"

Here we go. Her number one favorite question to ask. Sometimes I want to fire back, "Why don't you tell me how that would make *you* feel?"

"Of course I feel bad for him," I say. "I'm not a monster, you know. But if you're asking if I feel guilty because I'm out here and he's in there, I mean . . . there's nothing I can do about it, you know? It is what it is."

"Do you have any regrets?" she asks. "Things you wish you'd done differently that night?"

"I shouldn't have drank so much," I say, sounding more irritated than I mean to. "There. I said it. Happy?"

"Why do you think you did it?"

"Did what?"

"Drank so much?"

I uncross my legs. Cross them again. Why does this feel like I'm being interrogated all over again? "I don't know. Maybe because I wanted . . ."

"Wanted what?"

I roll my head from side to side. My neck pops. It feels good. "Wanted people to look at me the same way they looked at her. She was gorgeous in the vintage dress she'd picked out. It's pretty amazing when you can pull off something different like that. On some girls, it would look like they were trying too hard. But not Mirabelle. It was this brilliant red color, and when she walked in, I swear she lit up the room. Having to watch her and Mario hug onstage, and then dance after that? After they were crowned king and queen? It just . . . it wasn't fun. I'll put it that way."

"So you drank too much because you wanted to be prom queen?" she asks.

"No. I didn't want it. It wasn't like I was thinking *I wish they'd picked me.* Because they'd never pick me. Not in a million years. I'm the one they love to hate, you know that. The hating, I swear, it never stops. And Mirabelle? Well, she was one of the worst, if you want to know the truth."

"What do you mean?"

I try to figure out the easiest way to explain. "Do you remember the first time I came here?"

She nods. "Of course. You'd recently had that incident at the swimming pool and your father made the appointment because you really shut down after that."

"Do you know who owned the underwater GoPro? Because of her interest in marine biology, apparently?"

Besides the raised eyebrow on occasion, Tahni doesn't let a lot of emotion come through. A true professional, I guess, keeping a straight face through all the drama. So when she says, "Mirabelle?" she doesn't seem surprised or horrified. It's just like any other question she might ask.

"Correct."

"You sounded almost jealous before. When you described how she lit up the room. But now, I'm not so sure that's really what you were feeling. What do you think?"

I reach down for my mug and take a drink. "Don't you always say feelings can be complicated? Well, there you go. My emotions today are all over the map and I really have no idea which one I'll see next."

"I think that's understandable. I'm curious, though. You were so excited to be going to prom. I know the night took a really dark turn. But I'm wondering, did you have fun with Mario, mostly?"

I don't even hesitate. "Yeah. I did. He was super nice to me. Everything was good until they announced the king and queen. I still can't believe it. But man, did she seem happy about it. You should have seen the look she gave me while they . . ."

I don't finish. I realize I don't want to talk about that night anymore. I need to figure out how to move forward. That's what I need help with the most.

"What do you mean?" she asks. "What look?"

"Never mind," I say. "It's really not important anymore."

Her eyes drift down to the pad of paper she always has on her lap. "It's tragic. Two young lives, forever changed." She looks at me again. "If we assume he did it. Assume they have some kind of damning evidence. Which I think they must. Do you have any feelings about that?"

"Are you asking me if I feel guilty because I wasn't awake to stop it?"

"Hmm. Maybe. Do you?"

I grab a throw pillow with a colorful toucan stitched on it and squeeze it against my chest. "Didn't we already cover this? I feel a lot of things. It's complicated and all of that. Right?"

"Do you think he's capable of it?" she asks. "Of . . . killing someone?"

"No."

"You sound pretty sure," she says.

"Well, first of all, he asked me to go to prom when he hardly knew me. I'm pretty sure my dad and his mom played a part in it, but whatever. He didn't have to do it, but he did. Second of all, he cleaned the inside of his truck. He wanted it to look nice. Smell nice. For me. The guy is so thoughtful and caring. Like, he really seemed concerned about me. He was so patient with me. Understanding beyond belief. That doesn't sound like a murderer, does it?"

She doesn't answer me. Which happens a lot. I'm the one who's supposed to be answering the questions. Not her.

"So how's school been?" she asks. "Since it happened?"

I groan a little. I can't help it. "I tried to go yesterday, but if people hated me before? They *really* hate me now."

"Well, they don't know your story, right? All they know is you were with him. Maybe you need to take some time to explain to people what happened."

"They don't care about my story. Trust me."

"You still have a few more weeks until graduation. You have to figure out how to deal with them somehow."

I squeeze the pillow tighter. "I'll just ignore them. Like always. Or beg Daddy to let me switch schools. I'm actually thinking of talking to him about that tonight. Can you help me figure out how to convince him? That's the main thing on my mind right now, to be honest."

"It's really late in the year," she says. "Wouldn't it be easier to put in some effort and try to make it work where you are now? Can you maybe try? I know it's tough, but if you keep doing the same thing—"

I interrupt her. "I'll keep getting the same results. I know.

Don't you think I know? Look, I just want to get out of here. Start over. Start a new life. I'm tired of being me."

She raises her left eyebrow again. Two in one session. Wow. I've never gotten to three before. It's still early. Maybe today's the day.

MARIO

I miss food. Good food, not the garbage they serve here. I miss my soft, comfortable bed with crisp sheets, and the ability to choose how many blankets I want—one, two, five, ten. I miss being warm—at the same time I miss the ability to open up a window for fresh air if I want to. There is so much I miss. It's practically all I can think about and I feel like I'm falling into a deep, dark pit with no way out.

I tell myself to keep it together for my mom. As hard as it is, I have to pretend that everything's fine. She can't know that I feel like I'm barely hanging on. Otherwise, there will be two of us who can't sleep more than fifteen minutes at a time.

When Mom sees me, she has to smile through the tears as she picks up the phone receiver. I pick up mine and say, "Hi, Mom."

"Hi, sweetie." She wipes a tear away. "I'm sorry. I told myself I wouldn't do this. I'm just so happy to see you. But you look really tired, Mario. Is it hard to sleep here?"

"More like hard to sleep knowing I could be going to jail for the rest of my life. Or worse."

She scowls. "We have to believe that's not going to happen.

Do you like your attorney? Jon? He comes highly recommended. And every time I've spoken to him, I've felt like he truly cares. I think that's important. I don't want this to just be about him making a couple of bucks."

"How are you paying for this, Mom? For the attorney, I mean."

"Well, Ron and Carol are helping. And I realized last night as I was trying to fall asleep that I could probably take out a second mortgage. I'm going to go see the bank after I leave here." She chews on her bottom lip for a second before she says, "It'll be okay, Mario. We have to believe that."

The thought of her racking up bills to help me feels like a knife to my heart. "I'm so sorry, Mom. I wish—"

"No," she says waving a hand at me. "Please, don't. This isn't your fault. You hear me? This is a god-awful mistake and we just have to keep the faith that the truth will come out."

"Jon said he's gonna check on a possible witness. Someone who could help me. Help my case a lot."

Her eyes light up. "See? There's hope. There really is. Now, let's talk about something happier. Lucas came by to see me. He was very concerned. He's a good friend, which you already know. Oh, and Elana wrote a letter and I brought it along. Should I ask one of the guards to give it to you?" She reaches into her purse and pulls out an envelope and shows it to me through the glass.

"Throw it away," I tell her. "I don't want it."

She looks surprised. "What? How come?"

"Mom, please. Tear it up and throw it away. I mean it. I don't want you reading it, either."

She stares at me for a moment and then does as I ask. She tears it into small pieces and leaves them on the counter in front of her.

"What should I tell her if she asks if you read it?" Mom asks me.

"Tell her the truth. Tell her I wouldn't read it." I lower my voice. "They might call her in again. For questioning. We might have a new witness from the Little Country Store who saw me there that night and I don't want anyone to think we're working together to change our story, you know? See, we saw Mirabelle that night, Mom. We gave her a ride. But if we can prove I was at the Little Country Store, they may not have a case. It's better this way."

And I do my best to believe it. Even if I'm not so sure.

ZAIN

School on Tuesday.
A million conversations.
All about her.

Doesn't matter that she didn't go to our school. Doesn't matter that they didn't know her. All that matters is the shock and awe.

Stupid small town where gossip is just as fun as football. I want to scream at them. Scream at them to shut up because it's my goddamn girlfriend they're talking about.

I should just stay home. Ma went to work. Dollar Tree needs her to take people's dollars. Pop went to work. Hospital needs him to keep all those machines running smoothly. They trust me to do the right thing. And most of the time, I do.

I never paint on anything that belongs to someone. Never paint ugly things. Or cruel things. My goal from day one was to lift people up. To brighten someone's day. Brighten it up with Vino Purple and Chameleon Green and Tango Orange.

Paint with intention. With feelings that matter. Love. Honor. Integrity.

The morning is a blur. Pretty sure I slept through most of my classes. For lunch, it's Taco Time in Harry's van.

Shannon's got her head down, eyes on her phone, sitting shotgun while I sit behind them in the bench seat. She tells us, "There's a hashtag for her now."

"What is it?" I ask.

"#justiceformirabelle."

"They arrested someone," Harry says. "What more do they want?"

"Sounds like some people don't think he did it," Shannon says. She turns and looks pointedly at Harry.

Harry ignores her and pulls up to the drive-through. He gives our order. When he's finished, he checks the rearview. That is, checks on me. "Hey, man. You okay?"

"That'd be a big N.O.," I say, staring out the window. A bird is flying through the sky and I realize I feel about as okay as a wingless robin.

"You think they got the right guy?" Shannon asks, turning around to look at me.

"Wish I knew," I say. "Parker makes so much more sense. Especially if she broke up with him that night."

"Want to pay him a visit later?" Harry asks. "See what the guy has to say?"

My brain goes to colors, like it often does.

Furious Violet. Nope. Too pretty.

Slap Beige. Too plain.

Crush Pink. Probably not that kind of crush.

Knockout Brown. Hmm. Yeah. That sounds about right.

I shake my head. If that guy sees me coming? He better run like hell.

"What are you thinking, Harry?" I ask. "That we could get a confession out of him?"

"Maybe."

"How would that work, exactly?"

"Tell him who you are," Harry says. "What you had with Miracle. How much you loved her. Shit like that. Get him so pissed off he tries to kill you too, and in the process he confesses."

"You gonna wear a wire?" Shannon asks, nudging his arm. "Because you know if he confesses, you have to get it on tape."

He smiles. Grabs her hand and kisses it. "You've been watching *The Wire* again, babe?"

"Hey, it's a good show," she says. "So, it's our turn next. Prom, this weekend, I mean. But now, I'm not sure I want to go anymore. It's kind of . . . scary."

"Shannon, you know someone would have to go through me to get you, right?" Harry tells her. "I'm not gonna let anyone touch you. I swear."

"Man, that hurts," I say.

"What?" Harry asks.

"Like you're hinting that she's dead 'cause of me. And maybe it's true. If I'd gone to the barn like I was supposed to, she'd probably still be alive, you know?"

"Sorry," Harry says. "I didn't mean anything by it, I swear. You're not responsible and you shouldn't beat yourself up. Just trying to reassure my girl, that's all. Okay, we're almost up. Who's paying?"

Shannon grabs her backpack. Pulls out her wallet. "I've got it. Pretty sure it's my turn."

She hands him a twenty and he passes it to the lady at the window. When the bag comes, I get my food and my cup of water. Not very hungry but I know I should eat. I take a bite of the burrito. Can hardly taste it.

"Remember the first time we brought her here?" Shannon says. "We'd just finished that rainbow piece on the backside of that abandoned building downtown. We were starving. That's the first time I learned she was vegetarian. So weird how you can hang out with someone for months and not know such important things about them."

"I knew," I say.

We texted a lot. About all kinds of things. Long before we ever got together. I wish we'd done it sooner. We tried to deny what we felt for too long. But we both knew, I think. Or maybe I'm fooling myself. Maybe I was the only one who knew.

"Are you going to the service?" Shannon asks.

Suddenly it feels like I'm eating rocks. Big, heavy rocks that have taken up my entire stomach. "Yeah. I'll be there."

Shannon reaches back, her arm extended as far as it will reach. I take her hand and she gives me a squeeze. "I'm so sorry, Zain." Tears well up in her eyes. "I wish . . ."

She doesn't finish.

I wish she were still here?

I wish it didn't hurt so bad?

I wish there was something I could do?

I stuff my burrito into the bag and close it up. "Yeah," I say quietly. "Same." Because whatever she's wishing, I'm wishing it a hundred times harder.

LUCAS

get up and go to school. I try to ignore the glances that come my way all day long—some sympathetic and some accusatory. Lunchtime is the worst. It's always been me and Mario. I don't want to go off campus by myself. The thought of cafeteria food turns my stomach. I decide I'll just skip lunch today. Hang out in the library. That's definitely a first.

All I want is for the day to end so I can get over to Three Rivers and look for that van. Okay, I don't really want to do it. But I *need* to do it so I can get to the truth. That's all I want—the truth.

I take a seat at a table in the back of the library and grab a graphic novel from the shelf. *Fullmetal Alchemist.* One of Mario's favorites.

I haven't been reading for long before I hear, "Hi, Lucas." I turn and find Josh pulling up a chair next to me.

"Oh, hey," I say. "You actually came to school today?"

"Mom said I didn't have to. But being at home . . . it's hard. Today they're meeting with the pastor who's doing the memorial Saturday. I didn't want to be there. I didn't want to hear him pretend to care about my sister when he didn't even know her."

"Do you guys go to church?"

"No. Except at Christmas and Easter. You know. My parents have never been very religious. But suddenly, someone dies, and it's like you have to believe all the bullshit because to believe anything else hurts too much. Or something."

"Yeah" is all I can think of to say.

He's lost his sister. I've lost my best friend. Okay, I know it's not the same, because Mario isn't dead and dead is forever. But right now, with no way to see or talk to Mario, I think it must *feel* the same. Except I can try to save Mario. And seeing Josh and being reminded of all that he's lost gives me even more motivation to really try to do that.

"So I got into your sister's Instagram account," I tell him. "And I think I found something."

"I got in too," he says, his blue eyes suddenly wide open. "But what did *you* find?"

"There's a photo of two guys and a girl in front of Taco Time. I think she was hanging out with some kids from Three Rivers. Maybe painting graffiti with them. It makes sense, right? All the photos she took, the secretiveness, plus that fact that you caught her sneaking out at night."

"I thought the same thing. I just didn't know who she was hanging out with. So how do we find out who they are?"

"I'm gonna go try to find them. Today. After school."

"Lucas. Seriously? What are you planning on saying to them?"

"I have absolutely no idea," I tell him. "Any suggestions?"

"Gotta get their names somehow. Then turn them over to the police, maybe?"

"At this point, they've made up their mind. It's all on me now. I need to find out what they were doing Saturday night."

Josh shakes his head. "You make it sound like if one of them did it, they'll just come out and say so. I don't think it works that way."

Oh. Right. God, I'm such an idiot. What do I say to them?

I start brainstorming out loud. "What if I ask them to take me around and show me the pieces she did? Maybe I can tell them it's for an underground zine. Artists like that kind of stuff, right?"

"Zine? What's that?"

"A magazine, kind of. But . . . not as fancy. You seriously don't know what a zine is?"

"Nope. You think they'd buy it? Not sure I would."

"I don't know. The other option is to just tell them the truth. Tell them I'm trying to find the real killer and see if they want to help me. Hey, maybe if one of them seems really against it, that'll clue me in on who to look more closely at."

"Lucas?"

"Yeah?"

"I watched a lot of crime shows when I was in the hospital. Some nights, it was the only thing on that seemed halfway interesting. I'm thinking that if one of them did it and they think you're on to them, you need to be careful."

"Because I might be next?" I ask.

He blinks a couple of times. "Maybe?"

"I'll be careful. Trust me, Josh. Getting killed is about the last thing I want to do today."

I skip last period and head out. If I wait to go after school, I might miss them. When I get there, I drive through the parking lot looking for the VW van, which should be easy to spot. And it is. I'm such a dork that when I find it, I pump my fist in the air and yell, "Yes!" My best friend would be so proud.

I park in an empty spot across the row and down from the van a bit. And then I wait. Is this a stakeout? Am I really on a freaking stakeout? The thought alone just about gives me a panic attack.

What in the hell am I doing? I should be home, lost in a game of *Zelda*. Not here, ready to ambush people I've never met and accuse them of murdering someone.

I try to think of something to take my mind off the fact that I am basically stalking strangers who could be dangerous. My mind drifts back to when Mario and I went to lunch for the first time in his used but new-to-him truck. He'd bought it the night before, then came to school and asked Elana to go with him to the prom. We scarfed down our food and then hung out for a few minutes in the parking lot, neither one of us anxious to get back to school.

Instead of a stakeout, it was like an extended takeout.

"You are gonna get all the chicks now, bro," I told him as I ran my hand across the dash.

"Maybe not *all* the girls, but more than your sorry ass driving your mom's Prius," Mario joked.

"What? You don't think that car is hot? You're just jealous. Although I only get it Tuesdays and Thursdays while you can pick up cute girls twenty-four hours a day, seven days a week, you lucky man, you."

It was quiet for a moment. Then he asked, "Hey, Lucas? You think Elana's gonna like me?"

"What kind of question is that? Is the earth round? Does a bear shit in the woods? Can anyone actually stop at one handful of chips? Hell yes, she's gonna like you. What's not to like?"

"I don't know," he said. "I guess I'm just nervous."

"About what?"

"Messing up. Saying the wrong thing. Kissing her badly." He paused. "I think I need a lesson, maybe."

I put my hands out in front of me and waved them frantically. "No, Mario. You know I love you like a brother, but no. That is not going to happen. Not in a million years."

He reached over and slugged my arm. "I wasn't talking about *you* giving me a lesson. You think that shit's on YouTube?"

"Oh, yeah," I told him. "Dude, everything's on YouTube."

"Because what if she wants to kiss me?" he asked.

"Gee, let me think on that." I leaned in and yelled, "Then you KISS HER!"

It made him smile. It only lasted a second, though. "I have no idea what I'm doing. Why'd she even say yes?"

"Stop it, Mario. You're worrying for nothing. You and Elana are gonna have an awesome time. And if she kisses you, you'll nail it. I have every confidence in you."

See, here's the thing: that's exactly why I have to keep digging, no matter how much I hate it. Because the truth is, Mario Woods is one hundred percent a kisser, not a killer.

Now the hard part—to prove it.

PARKER

Tuesday's no better than Monday. In fact, it might even be worse. It feels like Mirabelle is already starting to be old news. And I don't want that. I don't want her to be old news, ever.

Everyone's focused on Mario. Talking about him like this is some sort of big celebrity case. Is he guilty or innocent? What evidence do they have against him? How did Elana get off while Mario may have to be in jail for the rest of his life?

By the time I get home, I just want to go to bed and sleep until tomorrow. At least the news crews have moved on, so I don't have to fight my way through them just to get to my house.

Grandma's in the kitchen pulling out a pan of brownies. The house smells delicious. "Thought I'd make you a brownie sundae," she says. "How's that sound?"

"Good. Thanks, Grandma."

"I'm sure it's not easy being there. At school, I mean. Without her."

"It's hell," I mutter as I take a seat at the kitchen table. "Sorry."

"No need to apologize," she says. "I'm sure it is." She pauses.

Sits down across from me, but she doesn't look at me. She stares at her hands, folded in front of her. "Parker, I want to ask you something."

"Grandma, please don't do this."

Now she looks at me. "It's just you and me here. I love you and you are safe with me. And I just want to make sure you stay safe, you see?"

I shake my head. My voice is almost a whisper. "You don't think I'm capable of something like that. Of . . . killing someone. Do you?"

"You said so yourself: you were highly intoxicated, trying to numb yourself from the pain. So I just want to hear it from you. That you were here all night, asleep on the couch."

I honestly can't believe she's asking me this. How is it possible that she has even a speck of doubt as to where I was that night? The fact that she's questioning my story, questioning my integrity, questioning the kind of person I am, makes me want to cry. But can I really blame her, when I'm questioning everything too?

She continues. "I'll stand by you no matter what, Parker. I hope you know that. I just want to hear you say it."

I put my elbows on the table and rest my forehead in my hands. I know I have to tell her the whole truth. "I don't remember," I say, and I watch her face contort with worry. I quickly keep talking. "I'm ninety-nine percent sure I passed out on the couch and somehow made it up to bed before morning." I pause. "I loved her, Grandma. I wouldn't hurt her. Ever."

She hesitates for a second and then pats my hand. "Okay.

Thank you. I just wanted to make sure there wasn't anything you were keeping from me. I felt it was important the two of us talk about it and get everything out in the open. That's all."

It still doesn't feel great, but I guess I can understand. "Okay. I get it."

She stands up. "Oh, one more thing," she says and pulls my lost phone out of her pocket. "I found this in the couch cushions."

She sets it on the table in front of me and it feels a little like a lifeline. At least this is one mystery solved.

"Now, let me get you that sundae. Do you want caramel or hot fudge on your ice cream?"

I smile. "Can I have both, please?"

"Absolutely."

As hard as all this is, it would be so much more difficult without my grandparents around. Definitely something to be grateful for.

HARRY

'm about to climb into the driver's seat of my van when I hear quick footsteps on gravel and a voice calling out, "Hey, wait! Hold on."

I turn and see a dude jogging toward me. A dude I don't recognize. At all.

"Thanks," he says when he gets close enough. He takes a second to catch his breath. "I really need to talk to you."

"Do I know you?" I ask.

"No. I'm Lucas. I go to Willow High. I was a friend of Mirabelle's. She mentioned you to me once. And I just, I want to make sure you know about the service on Saturday."

I nod. "Yeah. We know."

"You gonna come?" he asks.

"Yeah."

"Anyone else coming with you?"

Something about this seems strange. I can't put my finger on it. The kid looks nervous. He's sweating profusely and whenever he speaks, one of his eyes kinda twitches. "My girlfriend, Shannon. And Mir's, um, I mean, another friend of ours too."

"You guys hung out a lot, right? Painting or whatever you call it?"

"Yeah. She told you about that?" I get a chill down my spine. This isn't right. This guy's not legit. Mirabelle didn't tell anyone about us. She never wanted anyone to know what she was doing with us, or that she was even with us at all. It could get back to Parker and she knew he wouldn't like it. Even before Mir and Zain got together, she didn't want anyone to know. They wouldn't understand, she said.

Who knows what the hell he's really trying to get, but he's not getting it from me. I turn and open the door and jump in my van.

"Wait!" Lucas yells as I throw my pack on the floor of the passenger side. "Wait, please. I'm just trying to figure out what happened that night. My best friend is in jail, but he didn't do it! You don't know Mario, but I do. He's the nicest guy in the world. There's no way he could have done it."

I'm about to put my keys in the ignition when I remember our earlier conversation. The hashtag #justiceformirabelle pops into my head. A lot of people think they've arrested the wrong guy. If that's true, the killer is still out there.

I cared about Mirabelle. She was one of my best friends. The last thing she would have wanted was for some random guy to suffer for something he didn't do. Not to mention that the right person should be punished.

I roll my window down and look at this kid in his graphic tee, plaid shorts and gray Chuck Taylors. He looks harmless. And a little pathetic. If anyone could use some help, it's probably him.

"I have an hour until I have to get to work," I tell him.

"Where do you work?" he asks.

"Plaid Pantry. If you want to come along, I need to grab some food before my shift starts."

He doesn't even answer. Just trots over to the passenger side and jumps in.

"That's perfect, man. Where are we eating?"

I start up the van. "Subway has that special going on. Any footlong—"

"For six bucks," he interrupts. "Yeah, yeah. That sounds good." He stares at me. "I actually don't know your name. I found you because I got into Mirabelle's Instagram account and saw your van. When her brother told me she was sneaking out at night, I knew I needed to talk to you. Sorry I lied earlier."

I sit there, letting the van warm up. You have to let old VWs warm up. Things really don't go well if you don't. "I'm Harry." I hold out my hand and he shakes it. "Nice to meet you."

"Thanks for being cool about this."

"So you're not here because you think we might have had something to do with it. With her murder, I mean. Right? Because we wouldn't do anything like that. We all loved her. A lot."

"How did you guys, like, find each other?" he asks.

I stare out the window, going back more than a year ago. "She came across us late one night. Working on a piece. Told us she was a big fan of our work. And she just asked, straight up, if she could join us."

"And you let her?"

"Well, we talked to her for a while. Got to know her. She seemed to have this beautiful, artistic soul, you know? We got her number and told her we'd discuss it. And we all agreed it felt right."

"Did any of you talk to her Saturday night?" Lucas asks.

"You're sounding very much like a detective," I tell him. "Is that what you want?"

"Uh . . . no. I don't think so? I just want to help my friend. That's all, I swear. Maybe you guys know something that could help him."

I put the van into reverse and hit the gas. It sputters out of the parking spot.

"Here's what I know. Shannon was out of town. I was working. And Zain was at home with his parents and some of their friends. I think Zain texted her a little bit. But it was prom night, so . . . you know."

"Out of the three of you, who was she closest to?" he asks.

"Oh, that'd be Zain. One hundred percent."

It's quiet as I pull out onto Main Street. I'm guessing he's working hard to put it all together.

"Were they, Zain and Mirabelle, like, um . . ."

"I think the phrase you're looking for is *romantically involved*. And yes. They were."

"But—"

"She had a boyfriend," we both say at the same time. "I know," I say. "She kept promising to break up with him. Parker, I mean. Have you heard anything about it? We're wondering if she finally broke it off Saturday night. Zain thinks she did."

"Yeah," Lucas says. "She did break up with him. After Parker brought her home. That's what Mirabelle's brother, Josh, told me.

Hey, do you think Zain would want to come to Subway and talk for a few minutes while we're there? I'd really like to know what his texts from Mirabelle were like that night."

"Let's see, he works Wednesday through Friday after school and most Sunday afternoons at the used-car lot, detailing cars. So he's probably just heading home today, since it's a day off for him." We stop at a light and I quickly text him. The phone buzzes a few seconds later.

"He'll meet us there in ten," I tell Lucas.

And I think how strange it is that I feel like I'm suddenly in the middle of a new season of *True Crime*. Shannon would eat this shit up. Before the light changes, I text her too.

#justiceformirabelle? Hell, yeah. Looks like we're on it.

ELANA

After my appointment with Tahni, I stop in at my favorite little boutique in town, Polka Dots and Pearls, for a little retail therapy. I buy a new pair of jeans and two blouses. I grab some lunch at The Taco Stand nearby and then, as I'm heading home, I decide to make a detour. Mario's mom should be home by now, and I'm dying to know how her meeting went.

She greets me with a hug. "So good to see you. Please, come in."

"I won't stay long," I tell her. "I was just wondering how it went."

She leads me to her teal sofa and we take a seat. "It was fine, I suppose. He looks tired. And sad. But we had a nice visit, and I'm thankful for that."

"Did he read my letter?" I ask.

"Oh, no, honey, I'm so sorry. He was worried about how it would look. He asked me to rip it up and throw it away."

Of all the things I might have been expecting her to say, this was definitely not one of them.

Just then, the phone rings. She checks the caller ID and then turns to me. "Hold on a second."

I listen as she talks.

"Hello? No, I'm sorry, he's not here. He's, um, out of town for a while. I'm his mother, can I help you? Oh. I see. Well, um, something happened and so I'd like you to just send me the bill. Yes, yes, I understand. Do you have our address? Correct. That's the one. Okay, thank you."

She hangs up and looks at me. "His tux. They called to remind him that it's overdue and needs to be returned."

"Oh, no. You'll have to pay for it?"

"Yes. It's fine. Trust me, it's the least of my worries right now. Anyway, where were we?"

"You told me that Mario asked for my letter to be thrown away? Which seems weird to me. He wasn't even curious about what it said?"

"I can't speak to that," she tells me. "I'm sorry. But I'm sure he knows you feel bad about everything. I hope you aren't blaming yourself, Elana. It's not your fault. His attorney seems really nice, thankfully. Although I realize competency is more important than pleasantries. Still, I want Mario to feel cared for, you know?"

"Has he said anything else about the case? Anything good or bad?" I ask.

"Apparently his attorney is checking on a possible witness. Someone at the Little Country Store who could vouch for Mario? He didn't go into a lot of detail. Have you heard anything about that?"

I shake my head. "No. I haven't." I stare at her. "Is that all he said? About the case?"

"I believe so. To be honest, I tried not to talk about it too much. I figured he'd like to think about other things for a change."

219

I get to my feet. "Yeah. You're probably right. Well, I should probably get home. I need to get caught up on homework. My teachers emailed me some readings and assignments. I think I have to try to go back to school tomorrow."

"I know it must be hard," Ms. Woods says, standing up and rubbing my arm. "Hold your head high. Don't let them get to you. In time, the truth will come out. We have to believe that."

"Take care," I tell her as I walk to the door.

"You too," she says.

I get in my car and drive away. But I don't go home. There's one more thing I have to do.

ZAIN

Harry and the kid from Willow High are at a booth, chowing down on sandwiches.

"Hey," I say as I scoot in next to Harry.

Harry waves his hand back and forth between the two of us as he says, "Zain, Lucas. Lucas, Zain."

Lucas wipes his mouth and hands before he says, "Hi. Thanks for coming."

"Is Shannon coming too?" I ask. "Should we wait?"

Harry talks with his mouth full. "Couldn't make it. Just us three."

"So what's up?" I ask. "Is this about Mir?"

"Yeah," Lucas says. "Kind of. Mario's my best friend and I know he's innocent. Like, I've never been surer of anything in my life. But the police seem to believe they've got their guy, so I'm doing some digging on my own. Trying to figure out what happened that night."

"She broke up with him, Zain," Harry says, looking at me. "Just like you thought. Mir finally broke up with Parker. Lucas talked to Mir's little brother who heard about it from Parker's grandma."

"You sure about that?" I ask Lucas.

Lucas nods. "Yeah. I'm sure."

I don't know whether to laugh or cry. She did it. Took her own sweet time. But she did it. Just like she promised.

If only I'd gotten to her afterward. What might have been? A kiss in the dark. "I love you" whispered back and forth, wrapped in moonlight and stardust. An artistic masterpiece, just the two of us, ready to tell the world.

Finally we would have been free. Free to be the couple we'd wanted to be. I lean back, cross my arms across my chest and tell myself to breathe.

"You all right?" Lucas asks.

I shake my head and look out the window. People coming and going like it's just another day. Buying groceries. Picking up kids. Making dinner plans. How can the world keep spinning without her in it? I don't understand it. Not at all.

"Look, I'm really sorry," Lucas says. "I can tell you're hurt. But I guess, um, what I'm wondering is what she said to you Saturday night. In her texts. Did she say anything about Parker? About the party? Anything that might give us any clues?"

When I look at him again, I have to wipe away the tears. Can't keep them in. Haven't cried once. Until now.

What color is grief, I wonder?

Decay Gray, maybe.

"She asked me to come meet her," I tell them. "At our sunflowers. Said she had something to tell me. Something important. And I said I'd come, but then I couldn't get away. I had to cancel on her. Man, it killed me to do it, too. And now . . . If I'd met up with her? If I'd figured out a way to get there? Maybe she'd still be here."

"Don't do that to yourself, Z," Harry says. "It's not your fault."

It's quiet for a moment. Then Lucas says, "Do you think you could take me to the sunflowers?"

Harry burps as he pushes his plastic plate away. "I'd love to, but I can't. Duty calls."

"What are you thinking?" I ask Lucas. "You think I'm lying? Think I went out there when I just said I didn't?"

"No!" he says, a little too emphatically. "I just want to see it. The painting. The barn. The place."

"You want to look for clues, don't you?"

He shrugs. "I guess we could, if you want. Mostly, I'm curious. That's all."

I stand up. "All right. Let's go."

DETECTIVE GREEN

lead Elana into one of the interrogation rooms. Before we came in, I turned the equipment on. I have no idea what she wants to tell me, but whatever it is, I want it on tape.

"Take a seat," I tell her. "You want anything? Coffee? Water?"

"Um, no. I'm fine. This shouldn't take long."

I sit across from her. "All right. What is it? What's so important you wanted to see me?"

She bites her lip before she says, "I didn't tell the whole truth earlier. When the other detective questioned me."

"You don't say?"

"I was scared, you know? And I didn't want anything to happen to Mario. But now . . . now that time has passed and I've had time to think about it, I've realized I need to speak up. Do the right thing."

"Do the right thing?"

"Yeah. That's why I'm here. So can I tell you?"

"Please do."

"After we left the party, we found Mirabelle on the side of the road. Her car had broken down. Mario got out and offered to fix it, but she didn't want him to. She wanted a ride up the road. So he told her to get in and sit in the seat with me. Mirabelle didn't want to do that, though. Said we were on a date and she didn't want to ruin it. So she climbed in the back."

"Okay. Go on."

"When we pulled up to some property with a rickety old barn, Mirabelle showed us this beautiful piece of artwork. Big, bright sunflowers. It was really something. Anyway, she said she was meeting someone there. Mario said we'd wait with her. Until the person she was waiting for got there."

She fiddles with a ring on her middle finger. It's silver. Thin and wavy. But she keeps talking. "What you have to understand is that I was *so* tired. Like, I could hardly keep my eyes open. I'd had too much to drink and I just . . . you know. So I put the seat back as far as it would go and I fell asleep. He must have driven while I was sleeping, because next thing I knew, the truck was bouncing up and down slightly. I looked over but Mario wasn't in the driver's seat. I turned around and he was . . . he was pulling her out of the back of his truck. And then . . . god, it's so upsetting, even remembering it."

"Just tell me. What happened next?"

"Mario threw her in the ditch."

"What'd you do?"

"What do you think I did? I screamed. I screamed so loud. And he came running over and told me I had to be quiet. That he'd take me home, but I had to stop screaming.

"When he saw headlights coming, he told me to pretend I was passed out. That he'd do all the talking. He said, 'This right here is all I know. I found her like this. That's the story. Got it?'"

"You didn't see him do it?" I ask her.

"No. But it was just the two of them there by the barn. A while later, he's throwing her body in the ditch. It's pretty obvious, right?" She starts to cry. "I'm so sorry I didn't tell you before. I was just so scared. I didn't do anything to help him. I swear. And I hope by coming clean now, I won't be charged with anything."

"You didn't happen to make an anonymous call, did you?" he asks me.

I hesitate a second. But I decide there's no reason to hide it. "Yeah. I did. You don't know what it's like, living with the guilt of what happened."

"The guilt of what happened?" he repeats.

"I mean, not telling you what I saw. What I know."

"Well, you should have told the truth in the first place and saved us all a lot of time and effort. It's serious, what you've done. Lying. Changing your story. But if you'll testify on the stand, I can probably help you. Can you do that for us?"

She wipes her face with the back of her hands. "Yeah. I think so. I mean, it'll be hard. But it's the right thing to do, isn't it?"

I want to tell her we haven't found Mirabelle's cell phone, but we did discover some texts between Mario and his friend Lucas. Mario was clearly angry at Mirabelle that night. The texts show that. I want to tell her that with the prints and her testimony, we now have a rock-solid case. But I don't, because that's not the kind of thing you say to a witness. All I can do is smile as I say, "Yes, it's absolutely the right thing to do."

LUCAS

I stare at the sunflowers. They're mesmerizing. I think it must be one of the most beautiful pieces of art I've ever seen. Yellow and black and brown against the chipped and faded red paint. The barn is set back from the road, in the middle of a grove of big oak trees. If you're driving by and you're watching the passing scenery, you get a glimpse of the art. I wonder how many people see it and turn their car around because their curiosity gets the best of them. I'd turn around, that's for sure.

"All four of you did this?" I ask.

"We did," Zain says. "But they were Miracle's idea. Her favorite flower."

"Miracle? Why do you call her that?"

He shrugs. "To us, that was her name. It fit her. Fit us. The miracle we didn't know we needed until she was a part of us."

I can't help but study him. He's so different from clean-cut Parker. Zain's got a cool fro-hawk happening. He's wearing jeans with holes in them and a gray, baggy shirt that looks like it could use a good washing. I'm not judging. Just observing. Thinking about how different the two men in Mirabelle's life are from each other. It's striking how different.

On the way here, Zain told me he'd only dated a couple of other girls before Mirabelle.

"One of them I met at art camp. Man, that was one strange chick. She went to your school, too. After that, I swore off any girls from Willow High. Thought maybe there was something bad in the water over there. But Mir, she got under my skin. There was no way to be around her and not be happy. I told her once maybe she was a unicorn in a previous life, because something about her sure seemed magical."

"You didn't mind she was with someone else?" I ask.

He pinches his lips together like he's trying to keep himself from swearing. "Oh, I minded. I minded a lot. Almost broke up with her because of it."

I look around at this spot that feels so peaceful and lovely now, but would have been the perfect place to commit a crime in the dead of night. No one around for miles and set back a ways from the road. What if Zain was pissed about Mirabelle going to prom with her other boyfriend? What if she'd told him she couldn't break up with Parker, but then changed her mind, except Zain didn't know that? It seems like he has much more of a motive than Mario would, or even Parker, since Parker probably didn't even know about Zain.

A chill goes down my spine as I think about the delicate situation I now find myself in. If Zain suspects for even a second that I'm on to him, there may be another murder in the town of Willow. As much as I want to help my friend, I suddenly realize this definitely wasn't the smartest move, coming out here with him alone.

Zain looks around. "So you think this might have been where it happened?"

I gulp. "It kind of makes sense, doesn't it? She was headed here, to meet you."

"So you want to look for clues or what?"

"Sure. If you're up for it."

"And what am I looking for, exactly?"

"I don't really know. Anything out of the ordinary, I guess? Anything that might let us help Mario."

"Okay."

He walks closer to the barn, his eyes on the ground. I hesitate, wondering if I should turn my back to him. But he seems pretty occupied, so I go in the opposite direction, my senses on high alert and my hand tightly gripping my car keys in my pants pocket. It's all I've got if I have to defend myself.

It rained a little last night, so the ground is damp. Hard to find any footprints. I walk around to the other side of the barn and look out at a big open field with overgrown grass. In the distance there are more trees and, among them, a decrepit white house abandoned years ago. Hard to believe someone lived here once. And I can't help but imagine Mirabelle here, all alone, trying to defend herself from someone trying to hurt her. Did she scream? Did she put up a fight? Or did he catch her by surprise so she didn't have time for any of that?

We walk around for an hour. Maybe more. I start to wonder if I'm way off about Zain. He seems to really be trying to find something. If he didn't want us looking, seems like he would have tried to convince me to leave a long time ago. Eventually, I'm the one who calls off the search. I told my mom I was studying at the library but I'd be home in time for dinner. It's already six and I'm going to be late as it is.

"Sorry we didn't find anything," Zain says as we walk toward the Prius. And there's something about the way he says it that makes me believe him.

I kick at a rock. It bounces along the ground and lands on a small mound of dirt. I stop and stare at it. All around us, the ground is flat. Except there. In that one little spot.

I go over and look closer. And then I bend down, and I move the dirt with my hand. It moves easily. I dig down, deeper and deeper, the dirt cold and clumpy, my fingernails full of it. Until my hand hits something. Something soft. Silky.

I look over at Zain as I pull it out of the ground.

"What is it?" he asks.

I wipe the dirt away and hold it up for him to see. It's a small black handbag.

"Holy shit," he whispers.

Willow, OR (AP)—A man made his first court appearance today related to the death of Mirabelle Starr. Starr's body was found in a ditch early in the morning of May 15. Autopsy results show she was strangled to death. Police arrested Mario Woods in connection with the murder.

Prosecutors say Woods found Starr on Wessinger Road, not too far from where her automobile had broken down. He gave her a ride to a secluded spot and, while his prom date slept in the front seat, he strangled her to death.

"There was a trust relationship there. The victim had danced with him at prom and had no reason to suspect he would want to do any harm to her," says Assistant DA Marcia McDonald. "She got into his truck willingly, and it's sad that it took such a horrible turn just a short time later."

Woods, who is being charged with second-degree murder, pleaded not guilty. The judge set bail for Woods at two million dollars.

JANICE WOODS

It just keeps getting worse and worse. Mario's attorney called after the court appearance and explained to me what the bond means. Told me how much I'd have to have in assets in order to get him out. And I just don't have it.

"I'm still gonna pursue this other lead," Jon told me. "I haven't been able to track him down yet. But I'm not going to stop until I do."

"You really think he could help Mario?"

"Yes. If it's true, what Mario's told me, and we can find a witness to corroborate, we might be able to get him off."

"Is there anything I can do?" I ask.

"Not really. I'm sorry, but these things simply take time."

Time. Everyone goes on about their lives, doing normal things. Watering plants. Washing dishes. Scrambling eggs for breakfast. Arguing about politics. Meanwhile, my son sits in a cell for a crime he didn't commit. The minutes drag. When will it end? When?

"Why?" I ask him. "Why are they so intent on hanging this on Mario?" And then I begin to sob. The feelings of helplessness are overpowering.

"I'm going to do everything I can for your son," Jon tells me. "There's still hope. We need to hold on to it right now, all right? Hold on tight."

I said almost those exact same words to Mario yesterday and I want to believe them. But every minute that goes by, it gets more and more difficult.

One minute a young man is going to prom, one of the happiest nights of his life, and the next minute he's looking at a life sentence for murder? Life can change on a dime, my father used to say to me. You can't control what happens, but you can control how you respond to it.

The only response I can muster is to crawl into my bed. And that's exactly what I do.

LUCAS

Mirabelle's handbag.

Inside, her driver's license. Her car keys. Not one, but two phones. Her lipstick. A twenty-dollar bill. Her prom ticket.

And something else.

A wide silver scarf scrunched into a ball. A wrap, maybe? Is that what they're called?

Zain and I sit in a café, the contents spread out on the table in front of us.

"Zain?" I ask as I unroll the scarf. I study it. It's beautiful and looks expensive. I remember the photo I saw on Mirabelle's IG account. She wasn't wearing this or carrying it. All she had in her hand was a black handbag.

"Yeah?"

"I'm curious. Who was the other girl you went out with from Willow High?"

MARIO

After the court appearance, everything changes. Everything.

I kept hoping for some kind of miracle, but now I see there will be none of those. This is my life we're talking about.

And isn't my life just as valuable as anyone else's?

I have to do what's best for me.

When my attorney comes to see me, he says, "I'm still trying to get a hold of the cashier. I'm sorry I don't have better news for you yet. I do need to tell you that the prosecuting attorney has approached me to talk about a plea deal. I told him we're not ready for that yet. That I wanted some more time."

"I have to tell you something," I tell him, my stomach so upset I feel like I've eaten a three-day-old tuna sandwich. "I have to tell you what really happened."

Jon scowls. "I thought that's what you did yesterday?"

"I know," I say as emotions rise. I blink back the tears. "I'm so sorry. I should have told you the truth then. You gotta understand, I was scared out of my mind. Scared of what she'd do to my mom and me. What she'd say about me. She really messed with my head. I guess I thought . . ." I gulp. "I thought I was doing the right thing for everyone involved."

"Doing the right thing is telling the truth," Jon says. "Do you understand, Mario? This isn't a game."

"I know that now," I say. "Please don't come down on me so hard. I feel bad enough as it is."

"All right," he says pulling his legal pad out of his briefcase. "Tell me. Tell me what happened."

"Mirabelle climbed in the bed of the truck, just like I told you. And when we got to the barn, Elana and I both got out and studied the art. The graffiti art with those gorgeous sunflowers. Mirabelle stood there, shining her flashlight on them, and she said, 'Tonight, everything changes. I don't have to pretend anymore. I can finally be the person who painted these flowers with the love of my life.'

"She sounded so happy, you know? And then she grabbed me and started slow-dancing with me as she hummed a song. Then she said, 'Mario, we need a do-over. I treated you so badly earlier.' She'd apologized to me at the party, but she told me again how sorry she was for everything. Sorry for what she'd said. Sorry for how she'd acted. Sorry for pranking me."

"What prank?" Jon asks.

"There were worms in my crown. I mean, the prom king's crown. She admitted that she did it. She thought it'd be funny, but then, when the video went around, she realized it wasn't her best moment. I could tell she felt bad. She was kind of the class clown, you know? Always looking for the laugh, I guess. She kept asking me if I could forgive her. Said she'd been super stressed and she felt horrible taking it out on people who didn't deserve it.

"So yeah, I told her I forgave her, because really, how could I not? She hugged me really tight. And then she started humming again. She'd giggle. Hum some more. It made me laugh. That was the thing about Mirabelle. When life was treating her well, she had this, like, sparkle about her that made her so fun to be around.

"I wish I could remember the tune she was humming. I've thought about it so much. It's probably not important, but it's important to me, you know? Anyway, everything seemed really good. Until . . ."

"Until what?"

"Elana said she felt sick. She went over to the side of the barn and threw up. I tried to get her back in the truck, but she wouldn't have anything to do with me. She told me to go to the Little Country Store and get her some 7UP and some Pepto, if they had any."

"Wait a minute. You left Elana there with Mirabelle?"

"Yes. Mirabelle said it was fine. Said her friend would be arriving any minute and they'd watch over Elana until I got back. We'd used my truck's headlights up to that point so we could see. At first, I was worried about leaving them in the dark. But Mirabelle just laughed and pulled a bag out of the barn that had some cans of paint, a small flashlight, and a couple of headlamps. So I told them I'd hurry. And I did, too. I think I was gone a total of twenty minutes. But when I got back . . ."

I put my head in my hands. I know I have to tell him. I have to tell him every detail and get it out and then I have to do it again when it really counts. It'll never get easier. Never. Every waking moment, I see her body lying there, and Elana holding that silver scarf.

"When you got back, what? What did you see?"

"Elana, kneeling by Mirabelle's still body, rocking back and forth. Her eyes were blank. Empty. I screamed at her, 'What did you do?!' And you know what Elana said? She said, 'She's such a bitch. Didn't you see it? How could you not see it? Dancing out here like she's queen of the world. She didn't deserve to be that happy. Not after all the things she's done. I just . . . I couldn't take it. Not a minute longer.'"

Jon doesn't say anything. He lets me cry.

Finally, he says, "Did you help put the body in the truck?"

I nod as I wipe my face.

"Did you help dump her body in the ditch?"

I nod again. "I wasn't sure if Mirabelle's friend would be coming or not. It was just this instinct I had to get her out of there. Hide the evidence and put her somewhere with no clues or whatever. We did it so fast. I know it sounds horrible. And it was. I just . . ." I put my head in my hands and cry some more.

"Did you consider calling the police and reporting what happened?"

I tell myself to pull it together. I take a deep breath. "I didn't know what to do. Elana was wasted, and eventually she really started to seem sorry. Shocked and sorry. I don't think she meant to do it. I think she meant to scare her. Not kill her. Like, how could someone do that? She begged me to help her. To cover for her. And then she started threatening me if I didn't. When I saw the headlights coming toward us, it was too late to drive away. Elana pretended to be passed out. I pretended I'd just gotten there. That was our plan on the off chance we got caught. I thought we'd both be okay. I didn't think . . ." That's the problem, right there. I just didn't think it all through.

Jon scribbles more notes down and says, "We've got our work cut out for us, that's for sure."

"There's also stuff," I tell him. "Mirabelle's stuff. I buried it out there. Near the barn. That night, the cop noticed my dirty fingernails. I lied. Told him I was messing around with some guys outside at the party."

He nods. "Okay. Good to know." He leans back in his chair. "I wish you'd told me all this from the start, Mario."

"I know. Look, I was stupid, okay? Elana had me convinced that I was to blame. I should have stopped her from drinking so much. She kept saying it was my fault for leaving the two of them all alone in the middle of the night. The more she talked, the more I believed her. She said if I ratted her out, her dad would make life hell for my mom. He'd do anything for his little girl, I know he would, and all I could see were lies and misery for my mom. What if she couldn't ever get another job again? I just, I couldn't do that to her. But being in that courtroom, seeing how people looked at me, like I really am a killer? It dawned on me that one innocent person has already lost her life to this girl and I don't want to be another one. There are other places to live, right? If my mom has to move away and start over, I now realize she'd rather do that than see her son go to prison for the rest of his life."

"You may still do time, Mario," he tells me. "I'm sorry to say, but you tried to cover up a crime. That's no small thing."

"But if I cooperate?" I ask. "If I testify against her, and help them, won't that help me?"

"It might, but . . ." He sighs. "It's still bad. I'll do what I can, you know that. And maybe the jury will take pity on you, if we decide to go to trial. We'll just have to wait and see."

My heart feels like someone has taken an ax to it. "I didn't mean to hurt anyone. I really didn't."

Though I know it's too little, too late.

I'm sorry, Mirabelle. I'm so, so sorry.

DETECTIVE GREEN

What a difference a day makes. I now have new conflicting testimonies, new evidence including a burner phone with friends none of her family knew about, Mirabelle's phone records along with Mario's, a possible murder weapon, and a new witness who remembers Mario at the Little Country Store but doesn't remember the approximate time. What he does remember, however, is selling a kid in a tux some Pepto pills. The kid made a comment like, "Have to tell my date I was lucky I got the last box." And the witness replied, "Yeah, it's a big seller on prom night. That and condoms. Sure you don't want some of those too?" He said it made the kid laugh before he responded, "One hundred percent positive."

I want to say we had it mostly right. Halfway, maybe? But I'd be lying to myself. I wasn't even close to how it all went down. And it's killing me, if I'm honest. We should have slowed down. No, not we. *I* should have slowed down. It was on me, after all. I took the lead. But when a young, innocent girl is dead, people want answers. And they don't want to wait. Ultimately, it's our job to give it to them. People will never understand what the weight of that feels like. Never.

At least the result is on the money. Maybe that's all that really matters. I hope so.

When I get home, I go straight to Flora's door and knock. When she opens it, Percy the dog is on me like a rat on cheese. I grab the leash by the door and hook it onto his harness.

"Good evening," Flora says with her sweet and crooked smile. "How was work today?"

I answer the same way I always do. "Kept me on my toes, that's for sure."

"Well, Percy and I sure do appreciate you. You're a good man, Brendan."

"Thanks, Flora," I say. "That's nice to hear."

And after a day like today, I really mean it.

Willow, OR (AP) — Another suspect has been arrested in connection with the death of 18-year-old Mirabelle Starr, whose body was found in a ditch the morning of May 15 after she attended her school's junior-senior prom.

Elana Dexter, 17, was arrested Thursday afternoon by local police and charged in connection with Starr's death, according to a press release from Stephen Knight, spokesman for the Richland County Sheriff's Office.

Another person, Mario Woods, had previously been charged and held in the Richland County jail.

"New evidence has come to light thanks to information provided by the public as well as Woods to help us with this case," Assistant DA Marcia McDonald said. "I'm unable to share details at this time, but I want to assure the public we are confident that all parties responsible for the murder of Mirabelle Starr are now in custody."

Dexter's first court appearance will be Monday, May 23, at the Richland County Courthouse.

ZAIN

On the burner phone, the one Mirabelle used, there was a message she'd started writing to me but never got to send.

Didn't say much a few minutes ago because I was so disappointed you couldn't make it. We're waiting for Mario to come back from the store. I'll have him give me a ride home. I'm with his prom date. She says she knows you. Elana? She can't stop talking about you. It's weird. Didn't know you two

And then it stopped. Is that when it happened? While she was texting me, did Elana sneak up behind her and do the unthinkable?

I feel helpless. Miserable. Lost. Damn it all to hell. What am I supposed to do with all these feelings?

It's late and I can't sleep. Tomorrow's Friday. The next day's Saturday. The day we say goodbye. The day all the color drains from this world.

My phone buzzes. Surprised to see Lucas's name pop up.

You awake?

Yeah.

I want to learn how.

How to what?

Paint.

Why?

I just do. Can you teach me??

K. Meet me at Taco Time in 15.

I take him to an alleyway in Old Downtown. We've painted here before, but they covered it up not long ago.

I drop my backpack in front of us and open it up. Hand him his headlamp and put mine on. When we're suited up, I tell him, "Here are the colors I brought. Any idea what you want to do?"

"I heard at school Mirabelle was going to study marine biology in the fall. I thought maybe we could, um, paint the ocean?"

"That'll work. Brought a can of Blue Magic, which Mir loved."

"Perfect," Lucas says. "You bring any black? Because it might be cool to put something in that ocean as well."

"You bet."

We do the horizon in Milky Blue. The ocean in Blue Magic. And in the middle of it all, we paint a black whale's tail, standing tall and proud. Takes more than two hours to finish it. When we're finally done, we stand back and admire our work.

"It's like he's waving," Lucas says.

"Waving goodbye," I say.

"Or maybe 'see you later,'" Lucas says.

"Yeah," I say. "I like that. See you later." I turn and look at Lucas. He looks proud. Different from that kid I met a few days ago.

We put our stuff back in the pack and head out. The ride back to Taco Time is quiet. Peaceful. When I pull up to his car, he opens his door and says, "So I guess I'll see you Saturday?"

"Yep. See you Saturday."

He lingers for a second.

"What? What is it?"

"I'm just really sorry," Lucas says.

"So am I, man. So am I."

ELANA

I f only Mario had read the letter I wrote him.

Dear Mario,

I'm sorry this didn't go like we thought it would. It's not too late to change things. You know how she wanted us to leave? Mirabelle? And so we went to the Little Country Store to get some snacks while she stayed at the barn? As we were leaving, an old VW van pulled in. Remember? Pretty sure there were two guys in it. Friends of Mirabelle's from Three Rivers. Her graffiti artist friends. I know who they are because I followed them around sometimes at night. I loved watching them paint. I've always wished the one they call Zen would have invited me to become a part of their group.

But once again, I was the girl nobody wanted. Rejection is my best friend. My only friend, really. What I'd give to change that.

Why her and not me? That's what I've been wondering. God, how I've needed a group like that. People to watch out for me. To take care of me. While we waited there beside those gorgeous sunflowers, I thought, she doesn't deserve them. Maybe when she was painting she chose soft, beautiful words. But in the real world? Her actions and words burned like fire on skin. I think she loved hurting people like us. People who were "less than." Once upon a time, I thought I might take her place. I even picked out a name. Jewel.

Prince, Red, Zen and Jewel.

But now? We need to tell the detectives we saw that van. Do it, Mario. I'll do it too. With two witnesses, it'll be bad for them and good for us.

Hang in there,
Elana

I think it would have worked. I wish we could have tried.

JOSH

Mom and Dad decided to call it a "Celebration of Life." The church is packed. Mostly kids from school and their parents, from what I can tell.

They decided to have her cremated, so there's no casket to worry about. The front of the church has flowers and pictures of her. As people filed in to be seated, a slideshow played, set to the song "You've Got a Friend in Me."

Pictures of Mirabelle as a little girl. Blowing bubbles. Picking flowers. Eating cake. Eating spaghetti. Eating watermelon. It made people laugh. Good job, Mom.

The pastor did his best to comfort us after that. He used the words *hope* and *eternal life* so many times, I lost count. When he finished, a woman stepped up to the microphone and sang "Somewhere over the Rainbow." Everyone cried. I told Mom maybe we should go with something a little more up-tempo. Because who wants a funeral to be one long cryfest? But she said *The Wizard of Oz* was Mirabelle's favorite movie and nothing else felt right.

I've been thinking a lot about what happened. About what's right and what's wrong. I loved my sister, but she wasn't perfect.

Not by a long shot. Who is, though? She did some things she shouldn't have. Said some things she shouldn't have said. Mean things. But she didn't deserve to die. I wish she would have asked for help in dealing with everything. Maybe Mom and Dad should have seen she needed help. Maybe I should have told them that I suspected something was going on with her.

There are as many *maybe*s as there are stained-glass windows in this church. And none of them change the fact that she's gone.

Now the pastor steps up to the microphone again and says, "I'd like to open it up for people to share memories and stories about Mirabelle. Tell us how she touched your life. It doesn't have to be long. A sentence or two is fine, if that's all you can do. Or more, if you're up to it."

I glance around. Everyone's still wiping their eyes after that song. The awkward silence makes me uncomfortable. I shift in my seat.

Finally, Mrs. Winston, a language arts teacher from school, steps up to the mic. "Mirabelle was one of the best writers I've ever come across in my career. I asked her once if she wanted to be a writer someday when she got older. She gave me a funny look and said, 'Mrs. Winston, what do you mean? I'm a writer *now*!'" She smiles through her tears. "Well, I couldn't argue with that."

A few people chuckle and many applaud as she steps down. Next, my dad steps up there, white handkerchief in hand, wearing his new black suit Mom made him buy. "I'm Jerry, Mirabelle's dad. Thank you so much for coming. It means the world to us. And I want to tell you all how lucky I feel to have been in that bright, wonderful, artistic girl's life. Her birthday's coming up in

June, and boy, did we have big plans. She wanted to see the Grand Canyon." He looks up. At the ceiling. The sky. Because maybe she's there. Maybe she's listening. "We're still gonna go, baby girl. And you'll be with us. Right here." He puts his hand to his heart. "Always."

There's more sniffling and more rustling of tissues. I tell myself to go. To tell them what a great big sister she was to me. How she helped me through the worst time in my life, more than she probably ever knew. But before I can get my wobbly legs to stand, someone else goes up. I recognize him from Mirabelle's Instagram. He's Black with a cool haircut. He reaches into his dress pants and pulls out a folded piece of paper.

At the microphone, he says, "Mirabelle, I can't stop writing to you. Can't stop the intense feelings I have. I want to talk to you. Want to talk to you so bad. So I write. You understand. I know you do. And this letter, this one right here, if I'm brave enough, I'm going to stand up and read out loud to a whole bunch of strangers. People who will wonder who I am and why the hell . . ." He glances up briefly and says, "Sorry." Then he goes back to reading. "Why you were hanging out with me. But they don't know what we had, do they? Only we know that. Only we know the way we laughed at the stupidest, um, stuff. Only we know what magic feels like on a chilly April night with a sky the color of hope and endless possibilities. Only we know what it feels like when you don't have to say a word and you're so happy to be alive because your best friend is sitting next to you, holding your hand."

He stops and clears his throat. "If I could have one wish, it would be to see you one more time. Because I want to tell you the words I never said. I was waiting for just the right time, you know? For you to do what you needed to do. For it to be just you and me. Waiting, waiting, waiting. But no one told me time might run out. I wish I could buy you a dozen powdered-sugar doughnuts and a giant cup of hot cocoa with real whipped cream, sit you down, take your sweet, sweet face in my hands, kiss your freckled nose and tell you, 'I love you.' I imagine you'd say it back. Or maybe you'd say, 'What took you so long?' And I wouldn't have a good answer. Because we shouldn't wait." He looks out at all of us. "We should never, ever wait."

I catch a glimpse of Parker. He looks uncomfortable, but resigned, like in some ways everything finally makes sense.

Then I look over at Mom, wondering what she's thinking. I'm not sure what I expect to see. Anger? Disappointment? Confusion? But all I see is a grieving mom with tears in her eyes. Mirabelle was living a life we didn't know about. But as long as she was doing what she needed to do to try to be happy, maybe that's all that matters.

I remember the way Mirabelle looked in her sleeveless red dress with the full skirt. Radiant. Parker slipped the corsage onto her wrist. She pinned the boutonniere on his lapel. Mom took some photos. And then it was time for them to go.

Mom squeezed her hand. "Have a good time, honey. I love you."

Mirabelle smiled. "Love you too." She waved at Dad and me with her freshly manicured nails. "Love you guys!" she said.

And then she left to go dancing.

I hope she's dancing still.

Lucas: Hey. I was wondering

Zain: What?

Lucas: Can we do it again?

Zain: You liked painting, huh?

Lucas: Yeah.

Zain: You like chocolate donuts?

Lucas: I guess. My favorites are those little powdered sugar ones though

Zain: Shut up. Chocolate's the best

Lucas: Well, tbh, I'll happily eat either

Zain: Okay. You're in. See you Friday

Lucas: Should I come up with a name?

Zain: If you want

Lucas: How about Truth?

Zain: Good. Really good.

MARIO

When I walk outside for the first time, a somewhat free man, I don't move. I just stand there, looking up. The sun on my face. The breeze on my skin. I see my mom waiting for me. I wave to her and I think she knows. She knows I need just a minute, so I don't lose it when she finally gets to hug me. It's been a long time. To me, anyway. Now I understand why people say the wheels of justice turn slowly. I had to wait seven months just to be sentenced.

I pleaded guilty to being an accessory to murder after the fact, and in exchange for my testimony against Elana, I'm on probation for three years. There are fifteen conditions of probation I have to meet, and while it means I'm restricted in what I do and where I go, I'm beyond grateful I don't have to serve any prison time. Jon says I got lucky, since I could have served up to five years. When I went before the judge for sentencing, I read a letter I'd written, expressing my sincere remorse and basically begging him to approve my application for probation or alternative sentencing. I also asked Mirabelle's family to forgive me. They were there for the sentencing, and I was so scared when Mirabelle's dad chose to address the court.

What a relief when he told the judge the family forgave me.

After all, I wasn't the one who killed her. I just made some stupid decisions after the fact. He said the family didn't think a jail sentence was appropriate for what I did. Someday, with some distance behind us, I hope I can thank them for that in person. Without their support, I might still be locked up.

Elana goes to trial in a couple of months. Mostly, I try not to think of her. Once I'm done testifying, I'll try even harder.

I walk toward Mom and she runs toward me. She takes me in her arms and sobs, hugging me like it's gonna be my last one. Thank god it's not. I tower over her. And just like that, I'm back there, by the barn, laughing and slow-dancing with Mirabelle underneath the stars, towering over her too.

"I want to get you some food," Mom says when she finally lets go of me. "What sounds good?"

I smile. "Anything. Everything!"

"Whatever you want, it's yours."

"Mom?" I say as we head toward the car.

"Yeah?"

"After we eat, there's somewhere I'd like to go. Before we head home?"

"Sure. Anywhere you'd like."

"It's the barn Mirabelle painted. I want to see it in the daylight."

She nods. "Okay."

It'll probably be hard to go back there. But I figure it's the least I can do.

I've had lots of time to think about that night. About everything that happened. About the song Mirabelle hummed while we danced. I finally figured out what it was. As Mom walks me to the car under the bright blue sky, I hum it, softly. She looks over at me, tears in her eyes, and joins in.

"Here Comes the Sun" by the Beatles.

There are things I will always regret about that night. Things I'd do differently. And I know if Mirabelle were still here, she'd probably have regrets too. But dancing with her that night, under the stars, no ridiculous crowns in sight, isn't one of them. It's the one thing I want to remember.

The way she laughed.

The way she sparkled, like a star had dropped from the sky.

The way she seemed to love everyone and everything in that one brief moment.

Yeah. I want to remember that.

And I think . . . I think I want to live like that.

ACKNOWLEDGMENTS

This book is a work of fiction, and although I did my best in the way of research, I take full responsibility for any and all inaccuracies relating to the criminal justice system. A huge thank you to John Koch, a consummate professional, who answered a long list of questions and helped me more than any website possibly could. April Henry read a very early draft and provided helpful feedback, which I appreciate so much. Thanks to my editorial dream team, Ali Romig and Wendy Loggia, for their incredible guidance and help. You gave me just what I needed, and I appreciate you more than I can say. I also want to thank the cover designer, Casey Moses, for her excellent work. Thanks, as always, to my agent, Sara Crowe, for hanging in there with me through the ups and downs of this business. And finally, teen readers inspired me to write this book when I was substituting in libraries and saw how hungry they are for mysteries and thrillers. To the readers, as well as the teachers and librarians who help get books in their hands, thank you—you are the best!

THIRTY MILLION FOLLOWERS.
ONE DEAD BODY.

TURN THE PAGE FOR A PREVIEW OF THIS TOTALLY
ADDICTIVE THRILLER FROM UNDERLINED.

1

17 HOURS BEFORE

GWEN

"I swear to God, if we don't get it this time, I'm going to kill you both." Cami's face is red with exertion. She grabs my arm, her grip a bit too firm, and guides me through the moves again. "It's right, left, turn, and pose, okay?"

"So basically, how we've been doing it?" I mumble.

"How *I've* been doing it. You're still off," Cami snaps.

Cami's full name is Dolores Camila Villalobos de Ávila, but almost everyone calls her Cami, since, in her words, *Dolores is a name for a grandmother, not a TikTok star.*

She thinks she's in charge because she's the only one with "real" dance experience. She went to the School of American Ballet for two years, until she hit puberty and her curves became too pronounced for the world of classical dance. Cami's always patronizing me for not being formally trained or knowing all the proper dance terms—"*a frappé is not just something you get at Starbucks, Gwen.*" If I wanted to, I could be just as condescending back. It would be easy to knock her down a peg—remind her that I'm the one with eighty million TikTok followers, while she lags behind by more than half. That although she may know the "correct" way to count music, there's only one queen bee in this house: me.

But instead, I keep my professionally plumped lips sealed and nod along as she walks me through the forty-five-second dance for the tenth time. If I say anything now, things will just devolve into another fight, and she's right, we don't have much time left to get this right.

I honestly can't tell the difference between what I was doing before and what she wants me to do now. But she seems pleased with my improvement.

"All right, let's run it again." She turns to Tucker, who had been filming us but is now lying across the foot of Cami's bed, scrolling through Instagram. He's gone ahead and made himself comfortable, with his long limbs sprawled out. Tucker is six foot two, and from what I can tell, there's not been a moment in his seventeen years of life during which he's worried about the space he takes up.

"Huh?" He looks up from the phone. His eyes go wide as he registers Cami's expression: so grumpy she looks kind of constipated. "Oh, ready." He stands up and adjusts the backwards baseball cap on his head. He raises the phone and taps the screen to record. "Action!"

The music plays from TikTok, and we writhe and gyrate to the immortal sounds of the Pussycat Dolls.

"When I grow up / I wanna be famous / I wanna be a star."

Forty-five seconds later, Cami yells, "Cut." She snatches the phone from Tucker. "I think this is the one." She turns the phone so I can take a look. I watch us dance on the small screen. "See, I knew it wouldn't look off balance with just two of us."

"Yes, why apologize to your friend when you can just ignore the rule of thirds?" Tucker says.

"Exactly," Cami says, brushing off his sarcasm. She swipes through potential filters for our video. "And might I remind you that I'm not the only one Sydney's mad at."

Tucker bristles.

We haven't been able to dance in our usual formation—Sydney to my right, Cami to my left—since the big fight two days ago. Sydney stormed off that night, headed for her parents' house in the hills. She hasn't sent anyone here so much as a Snap or a text—let alone indicated she's ready to shoot TikToks with us again.

"Are you sure about the song?" Tucker changes the subject from his girlfriend's disappearing act. "You don't think it's a bit too on the nose?"

Cami shakes her head. "It's tongue-in-cheek, Tucker."

"What do you mean?" I say. Confused, I touch my own cheekbones, then the tip of my nose. Contour comes off on my fingers. "Does my nose look big in the video? Let me see again."

Cami rolls her eyes.

Tucker laughs at me. "Not literally noses and cheeks, Gwen," he says. "They're expressions."

"Duh, I knew that." I straighten my shoulders. "I was just trying to be funny."

"Sure, honey," Cami says with a look of pity.

Embarrassment burns hot in my chest. I hate when people think I'm dumb. People assume that since I'm seventeen, platinum blond, and basically as close to looking like Barbie as La Mer skin care, the Tracy Anderson Method, and Dr. Malibu

(Plastic Surgeon to the Stars) can get me, I also must be shallow. But I'm not. I'm actually quite smart, in my own way.

I may not know much about the sorts of things they teach in school, or what "on the nose" means, which everyone else does, apparently. But I know the right time of day to post an Instagram, which is different than the right time to post a TikTok. I know which camera angles work best for me, and I know to match an ironic sound with a thirst trap, so you don't seem too into your own looks. I know how to put out enough content to stay relevant without becoming overexposed.

And I thought up this plan. Everyone forgets that, because it was Sydney's parents who signed for the mortgage. But it was actually my idea to form the Lit Lair—to gather a bunch of teenage TikTok stars and move into a Malibu mansion to create content together. I thought that if we appeared in each other's videos, our accounts would all grow much faster than they would apart. And I was right. I recently learned it's called synergy—when two plus two makes five instead of four. But even before I knew the term, I knew it was a good idea.

When it comes to turning myself into a brand, I have a gift. As Paris Hilton once said, "Some girls are just born with glitter in their veins." That's me. I always knew I was meant for this life. Even when my mom and I were living in a cramped studio apartment and my bed was a pullout couch, I'd look at my secondhand Barbie Dreamhouse and just know I was meant to live in a place like that.

It may look like fun and games, us all living in this house together—swimming in the infinity pool, making up dances, playing pool in the dining room—but really, it's serious business. We have thirty-five million followers on the @LitLair_LA account. Plus, we all have our personal profiles, with at least ten million followers each (I'm the one with the most followers, and Sydney and Cami are always fighting for a distant second).

All these followers mean sponsorship deals, and not just with any random company—after all, we have our brand to protect. We work mostly with Fortune 500 companies. And my rate per post is at least $30,000. Since we moved into the house at the beginning of the summer, I've made more money starring in a series of sixty-second videos than most Hollywood starlets make for an entire film.

Not bad for a girl with no talent, as Kim Kardashian would say. And that's the blueprint, really. If you're going to monetize your personal brand, there's no better example than the patron saint of influencers out in Calabasas.

That's why lately I've been trying to diversify my portfolio. Things may appear perfect from the outside, but I'm terrified that one day I'll just be someone who used to be famous on an app most people have forgotten about.

Because, sure, TikTok is, like, the biggest thing in the world right now. But what if it goes the way of Vine or Myspace? So even though I currently have the most followers of any individual on the app, I don't want to just be a TikTok star. I want to be an It Girl. I want a makeup line, a lifestyle website, maybe a shoe collab. I want to publish a book made up mostly of my Instagram photos and have it hit the *New York Times* bestseller list. I want it all.

Some old dude once said, "The unexamined life is not worth living." This is how I know my life is worth a lot: it is examined by eighty million people every day. That's like, more people than the population of France. Having all these people caring about me and the way I dance and the clothes I wear, it makes me feel like my life matters. I don't ever want to lose that. I don't know who I would be without it.

But my mom, bless her heart, is no Kris Jenner. Since I got famous, she's spent her days playing tennis and drinking mimosas, not strategizing for my career. So I have to figure this out on my own. And with every comment below one of my videos from some troll saying I'm overrated, that I'm gaining weight, that no, I'm losing weight and must be anorexic, that my dance moves are too basic, that I am actually a conspiracy created by the Chinese government, or—most commonly—that I'm dumb, I can feel my fifteen minutes ticking by. And I worry they'll be gone before I can build something that will last.

Comments questioning my intelligence coming from strangers stress me out enough. I don't appreciate them from people who are supposed to be my friends, and especially not from Tucker.

"I guess you're lucky that you know everything about everything, Tuck," I say. I glare at him, thinking all the things I can't say with Cami here as a witness.

He flushes under my glare. "If you have the shot, then I'm gonna go get ready for tonight." He walks out of Cami's room and away from my rage.

Cami captions the post *Dynamic Duo* and adds the two-dancing-girls emoji. Then she presses a button and the video posts to @LitLair_LA and its thirty-five million loyal followers.

Within seconds, I watch on my own phone as the video begins to gather likes and adoring comments. But even so, watching the TikTok back, I must agree with Tucker. It just feels like something's missing without our other best friend dancing beside us.

"Syd will be back tonight, though, right?" I ask Cami.

"Of course," she reassures me. "She might be mad, but she's not stupid. She wouldn't miss Drake for the world."

I nod, but I'm not totally convinced. All I can think about is Sydney as she stormed out of the house, her Louis Keepall on her shoulder and her Away suitcase clunking on the stairs behind her. Her cheeks were stained with mascara, but what I remember most is her eyes. Because even though she was crying, she didn't look sad. She looked pissed.

I leave Cami's room and head down those same marble stairs, which are now soaked in Malibu sunlight. My perfectly manicured hand slides down the railing, and as I make my way downstairs, I hum quietly to myself, Nicole Scherzinger's voice still stuck in my head.

"Be careful what you wish for / 'cause you just might get it."

16 HOURS BEFORE

KAT

My father's side of the family has been in California since the gold rush. My great-great-great-great-grandfather raced across the country in a covered wagon and ended up somewhere near Fresno.

His first week in the state, he found a small nugget of gold. He grabbed the gold, left his sifting pan in the river, and went promptly to the town's only two permanent businesses: a saloon and a brothel. Within the month, the money was gone and he was back to searching for a glimmer in the California dust. He looked his whole life but never found more gold. He died completely broke; there wasn't even any money left for a proper headstone. His descendants have lived in central California ever since.

My mom tells this story like a warning. Her family has a very different history. Her parents immigrated from Jamaica. Her mom became a nurse, her father worked in construction. My mom grew up and became a middle school teacher. Theirs is a story of hard work, staying in school, working solid union jobs. An American dream, not of ephemeral gold dust and that intoxicating promise of quick riches, but of daily bread carved from steady work.

So you can imagine how it went when I told her about coming here. To this get-rich-quick-influencer-palooza mansion.

My TikTok started as something to do for fun. Everyone at school had an account, and my parents didn't care if I made silly short videos with my friends as long as I kept up my schoolwork. But for some reason, my follower numbers didn't plateau around two hundred, like most of my friends' accounts. My videos kept making it onto the For You pages of people I didn't know all around the world. I had a few videos go really viral—like I'm talking my phone crashed during AP History because a video got a million views in three hours. And then, all of a sudden, I had 150,000 followers, then 400,000 a few days later, and then . . . well, you know how exponents work.

I'd been making a bit of money—a few hundred dollars here and there to promote small businesses—when I got the DM from Gwen. She told me she was making upward of twenty thousand for one sponsored post, and that she would love to teach me how, and would I like to come live with her and her friend Sydney in SoCal?

At first my parents gave me one month—June. This could be my summer job, my mom said. But I needed to make at least $480 a week—the equivalent of what I would make working forty-hour weeks scooping ice cream or babysitting in Fresno. In the first month, I made $40,000. It went right into the college fund, of course, except for what I spent on rent and an allowance for food and new clothes. But I still shopped at American Eagle and Target. I certainly wasn't buying the latest Gucci with my income, like some of the other TikTok kids. And that was fine with me. The money just meant I could show my parents that what I was doing here was work and help me negotiate for more time. They agreed to let me stay the rest of the summer.

One summer making videos full-time. One summer in the now-famous Malibu mansion. And then I was supposed to go back, finish high school, take the SATs, and generally get on the path to a real, steady job that is definitely not being a comedian and relying on the whims of the internet to determine whether I boom or bust. As of today, I have three weeks left of living my dream.

My heart beats hard in my chest, my blood racing through my veins. The pool water slides off my arms with every slicing movement.

My Apple watch alerts me that I have reached my daily activity goal. But I want to do a lap or two more. The sun is bright, and I can feel it on my back as I swim. It's a beautiful day in Malibu.

I get to the end of the pool and flip, propelling myself back in the other direction, gliding through the water. I spot two wavy feet that have now appeared at the other end of the pool. Even though I am underwater, my cheeks twitch up in a smile. My limbs are tired, but I find a bit of energy I didn't know I had left and speed up to get to Beau faster.

"Hi," I gasp as soon as I pop up out of the water. I lift my goggles. Beau smiles down at me. He is shirtless and sweaty from his run along the beach. His wavy surfer-dude hair still somehow looks perfect.

"How was your swim?" he asks me.

"Good. I'm close to beating my record," I say. I pull my cap off and rub my temples where I know the cap and goggles have left weird, angry marks on my face.

"You didn't want to be part of Cami's video?" he asks.

"Believe it or not, I'm not a huge Pussycat Dolls fan."

"Ah, really?" he teases.

Beau knows I hate to do dance videos, and that it's mutually understood with that crew to just stay out of each other's way. Like me, he specializes in comedy TikToks. I'm the only girl in the house who doesn't focus on dance videos—I mean, except when I Renegaded to Bill Clinton's "I did not have sexual relations with that woman" testimony and captioned it *When everyone asked Joseph how Mary got knocked up.* I don't mean to sound all I'm-not-like-other-girls about it, because there are plenty of other girls whose TikTok accounts are about being funny, not just being cute and dancing. I'm just the only one like that who lives in this house.

Beau extends his hand and helps me out of the pool. I wrap a towel around my body. The sun is sinking toward the horizon, but the late-summer heat still hangs in the air, and the breeze feels good on my skin.

"I stopped in town on my run and saw this." Beau reaches into his shorts pocket and pulls out a bracelet made of black string and white seashells.

He holds it out to me carefully. "I thought you might like it."

I turn it over in my hand. "I love it."

"I know it's not *Cartier*," he says with an affected tone. "But it reminded me of your style."

I laugh at his joke. For the first few weeks after we moved in, Sydney would not shut up about this Cartier Love Bracelet her parents got her. She bugged me for weeks to make a video with her to the "I can't take it off" sound, and I eventually had to pull her aside and let her know that a video about a six-thousand-dollar bracelet wasn't exactly relatable to a teenage audience. That was the last time someone from the dance posse tried to make a comedy video.

I tug the seashell bracelet onto my wet wrist and smile up at Beau. "It's perfect," I say.

"Cool." He blushes. "I'm glad you like it."

For a moment, we just stand there at the edge of the pool, squinting in the sunlight, smiling like idiots. I'm still breathing hard from my swim, and I feel like my heart is beating in my ears.

"*What* are you two doing?" We are jolted from the moment by Cami, who's racing down the pool stairs in a dress and neon block heels. "Do you not understand that *Aubrey Graham* is coming here in one hour? How are you not even showered yet?"

"I was about to go up," I say.

"Golden hour is seven. Be in the foyer by six-forty-five." She says "foyer" the French way.

"Of course!" I say as I pass her. Beau and I giggle like little kids and race up the wet stone stairs to the house.

Upstairs in the girls' bathroom, I peel off my one-piece and step into the shower. This is my favorite part of the house. The whole back wall of the shower is glass—a giant window looking out to the ocean. The house is on a cliff and was designed with as many rooms as possible facing the ocean so you can enjoy the view from everywhere, even from the crapper, as my dad would call it.

I rinse off the salty water from the pool and breathe in the scent of my grapefruit body wash. I watch the waves crash onto the shore, and for the umpteenth time this summer, I think: *How is this my life?*

For as long as I can remember, there have been two Californias in my mind: The real place where I grew up, where I went to school and scooped ice cream and did homework, and the mythical California of Jack Kerouac's writing and Lana Del Rey's songs. It's the place where people chase glory: Hollywood dreams, Silicon Valley riches, and, yes, if you are like my distant relatives, literal gold in the ground. California is where you go so that something happens to you. Something big.

But I never felt like that was going to happen in Fresno. And now here I am. Where my idea of California and my reality finally collide. Watching the sun set over the Pacific as I shave my legs.

I towel off and head to my room to get dressed. There was a big fight over who got the best room when we moved in, but I just picked the one with the lowest rent, which means I have a view of the pool rather than the ocean. I pull the curtains closed so I can change.

I have no idea what to wear to meet Drake, so I decide just to put on what I would if someone's parents were visiting. My usual look but dressed up a bit more, to show respect. I pick out a yellow floral sundress and dab on a bit of minimalist makeup in front of my seashell-framed mirror.

On the vanity, my phone vibrates. *Call from Mom,* the screen says. We usually talk about once a day. But over the last few days, I've been dodging her. I know she wants to talk about plans for moving me back to Fresno, but I'm not ready to think about that yet. I'm still working up the courage to tell her and my dad that I'd like to take a year off school and stay here longer. I already know how they're going to react. I click the lock button to silence the call.

I grab a scrunchy to wear around my wrist as usual. But this time, I put it on my right wrist rather than my left, so as to not cover up my new bracelet. I spin one of the shells between my fingers. *It reminded me of your style,* Beau said.

I sigh. I've been crushing on Beau since we moved into the house. Before I met him, I saw some of his videos, so I knew he was funny and quite cute. But to know him in person was a whole different level. He's one of those people who can make the vibe of a room better just by walking in. His laugh is infectious, and his smile makes you feel like smiling, too. When someone is sad, he always knows what to say to comfort them. He's the kind of person who'll notice whoever at the party doesn't know anyone and is lingering at the edge of the room and go talk to them. He always knows how to break awkward silences and what songs to add to a playlist to bring up a waning mood. He just makes everything warmer, happier. He's like sunshine.

During the first week here, when everyone was nervous and competitive and constantly comparing sponsorship deals and video views, Beau just . . . didn't engage with that drama. He made his videos, and then he went surfing. He asked everyone if they wanted to go with, but I was the only taker. He patiently taught me how, even though it took most of the morning for me to stand up on the board. I was smitten by the end of the day, both with the sport and with the boy.

Sometimes I even think he might feel the same way. Like, we'll be in a group and I'll catch him looking at me even when it's someone else talking. Or he'll save the last piece of pizza for me. Small things like that. Then again, he's pretty much nice to everyone in the house and, really, everyone he encounters, so it's hard to tell if it means anything.

I know some of the people who watch our videos ship us. But others ship me with Spider-Man—not Tom Holland but the literal fictional character, Peter Parker—so, you know, it's hard to put too much stock in that.

I look down at the bracelet. That must mean something, right? I mean, you don't just get a bracelet for all your friends, right? Bracelets are for crushes, girlfriends, not just friends—

I'm barreling down this train of thought when I remember the concept of friendship bracelets. *Well, crap. Never mind.*

I take a deep breath and check my hair one last time before heading downstairs and into the fray.